PIZZA IS THE

Best Breakfast

(AND OTHER LESSONS I'VE LEARNED)

DON'T MISS ANY OF
MANDY BERR'S ADVENTURES!

DON'T WEAR
Polka-Dot Underwear
WITH WHITE PANTS
(AND OTHER LESSONS I'VE LEARNED)

* * *

A CAST IS THE
Perfect Accessory
(AND OTHER LESSONS I'VE LEARNED)

* * *

NEVER WEAR
Red Lipstick
ON PICTURE DAY
(AND OTHER LESSONS I'VE LEARNED)

PIZZA IS THE

Best Breakfast

(AND OTHER LESSONS I'VE LEARNED)

BY ALLISON GUTKNECHT
ILLUSTRATED BY STEVIE LEWIS

ALADDIN
NEW YORK   LONDON   TORONTO   SYDNEY   NEW DELHI

ALADDIN

An imprint of Simon & Schuster Children's Publishing Division
1230 Avenue of the Americas, New York, NY 10020
This Aladdin paperback edition March 2015
Text copyright © 2015 by Allison Gutknecht
Illustrations copyright © 2015 by Stevie Lewis
Also available in an Aladdin hardcover edition.
All rights reserved, including the right of reproduction in whole or
in part in any form.
ALADDIN is a trademark of Simon & Schuster, Inc., and related logo is a
registered trademark of Simon & Schuster, Inc.
For information about special discounts for bulk purchases, please contact
Simon & Schuster Special Sales at 1-866-506-1949 or business@simonandschuster.com.
The Simon & Schuster Speakers Bureau can bring authors to your live event. For
more information or to book an event, contact the Simon & Schuster Speakers
Bureau at 1-866-248-3049 or visit our website at www.simonspeakers.com.
Cover designed by Jessica Handelman
The text of this book was set in Arno Pro.
The illustrations for this book were rendered digitally.
Manufactured in the United States of America 0615 OFF
2 4 6 8 10 9 7 5 3
Library of Congress Control Number 2014956143
ISBN 978-1-4814-2962-7 (hc)
ISBN 978-1-4814-2961-0 (pbk)
ISBN 978-1-4814-2963-4 (eBook)

For the Wacky Wagners
WHO PROVE THAT THE BEST COUSINS
ARE ALWAYS FUNNIER THAN FICTION

Many Thanks to

ALYSON HELLER, EXCELLENT EDITOR AND
ACCESSORIZER EXTRAORDINAIRE,
CHARLIE OLSEN, AMAZING AGENT AND KING OF THE WAHOOS,
AND FAYE BI, TOP SPREADER OF MANDY'S MAYHEM.

ENDLESS APPRECIATION TO
THE ALWAYS FANCY-DANCY TEAMS AT
ALADDIN AND INKWELL.
YOU ALL ARE SOME OF MY FAVORITE PEOPLE IN THE WORLD
(AND NOT JUST MOST OF THE TIME).

Contents

CHAPTER 1

Glue Stick Stickup

IT IS NOT MY FAULT THAT THERE IS CHOCOLATE PUDDING IN Timmy's hair.

Mom says that it *is* my fault, of course. She thinks that just because I pulled the pudding cup away from Timmy, and it squirted on his face when I squeezed it, that this whole chocolate pudding thing is my problem.

But I promise that it is not.

"You said I cannot eat pudding for breakfast," I tell Mom, still holding the almost-empty pudding cup in my hand. She lifts Timmy onto the counter to sit and begins running a wet paper towel down his bangs.

"You can't," Mom answers.

"But Timmy was," I point out. "And that is not allowed."

"You're right, that's not allowed," Mom says. "But you had no business grabbing the cup away from him like that. You should've just told me."

"Then you would have called me a tattletale," I tell her, which I think is a pretty good point.

Mom sighs an enormous gust of breath—so enormous that the tippy-top of Timmy's hair blows a little from her nose wind.

"Timmy should not have been eating pudding for breakfast—do you hear that, Timmy?" Mom lifts his chin up to face her, and he nods his head, even though he is still licking chocolate from his lips. "But, Mandy, you did not have to intervene.

Next time—and there better not be a next time, Timmy—just come get me."

"So I should tattletale."

"Mandy," Mom says with a warning in her voice. "Enough."

When Mom's back is turned, I stick my longest finger inside the pudding cup and swoop up the last bite. Then I drop the cup onto the counter, because I am not cleaning up a three-year-old's trash. No way!

"Mandy eat pudding," I hear Timmy call then, and I whirl around on my heel to face him. He is pointing at me as Mom wrings his hair into wet tangles. "Mandy eat pudding too. I saw."

"Worry about yourself, Timmy," Mom says. "And, Mandy, throw that pudding cup away for me, please." I pick the cup back up in my hand and stomp toward the trash can, and I wiggle my finger through the pudding one more time, just to swipe up the last of it, before I toss it in the garbage.

"You're welcome, Timmy," I call, and he does not even say thank you for throwing out his trash, which I think is rude. I am pretty sure that if Timmy had to throw out my trash after I ate pudding for breakfast, I would have had to say thank you, so I stick my tongue out at him.

"Okay, I think it's all out now," Mom says, and she grunts as she hoists Timmy off the counter. But I think she should have left the pudding in his hair, because then at least the front of it would have been brown like mine. Not that I would like to look like Timmy, but I also do not like that he gets to have blond hair and I do not. At least the pudding would have made things even.

"You're going to be late for your bus, Mand," Mom says as she rinses her hands off in the sink.

"Mandy," I correct her.

"I know your name, silly," Mom says. "Mand is just short for Mandy. It's affectionate."

"I do not like it," I tell her.

"I thought you didn't like Amanda."

"I do not like that, either," I say. "I like Mandy. With a *y*. The *y* is the best part."

"You have a lot of rules, you know that?" Mom says, and she kisses the top of my head. "Skedaddle. Your bus will be here in two minutes. Remember your jacket. And be careful of the twins on your way out, please."

I trot out of the kitchen and Timmy calls "Bye, Mandy!" after me, but I do not answer him. The twins are lying on the living room carpet like blobs, looking at mobiles. I hold my nose as I step over them, because one of them always seems to stink like a dirty diaper.

I grab my book bag and open the front door before I remember.

"When is Paige coming?" I call to Mom.

"Tonight," she yells back.

"But what time?" Paige is my favorite cousin in the whole world, and I haven't seen her since last Christmas, which I think is way too long.

"After dinner. Grandmom is going to pick her up at Uncle Rich's house this afternoon," Mom tells me.

"And she is going to sleep in my room, right?" I ask. "Like a slumber party?"

"That's the plan," Mom answers.

"Wahoo!" I open the front door all the way and then slam it behind me, dragging my book bag along the ground as I gallop like a pony toward the bus stop.

Because if there is one thing that puts me in an excellent mood, it is Paige, because Paige is fabulous. That is her favorite word—"fabulous"—which is perfect because that is exactly what she is. Paige looks like a princess with very wavy hair and real pierced ears, and her lips are so pink that she always looks like she is wearing lipstick, even though she is not. Plus, Paige does not have any brothers or sisters, which is what I would like to have, except that sometimes I like to pretend that Paige is my sister. She would be a much better sister to have than the twin, because even though Paige is already ten years old, she never cares that I am only eight. Because I am her favorite cousin too, just like she is mine.

And favorite cousins are absolutely the best kind to have visit you.

"Psst." I lean against my desk and hiss at Dennis. "Psst, Freckle Face." I tap on the edge of his desk, which is now right next to mine. This is Mrs. Spangle's way of making sure that Dennis and I get along more than we argue with each other.

I do not think this plan is working out so well.

"What?" Dennis runs his hand over the top of his Mohawk. We are supposed to be creating maps of our neighborhoods with construction paper, but Dennis doesn't seem to be doing much more than petting his own hair.

Though I have always wondered what the top of a Mohawk would feel like, if I am being honest.

"Are you done?" I point to his paper, which looks even worse than the artwork Timmy makes in preschool.

"Yeah."

"Can I use your glue stick?" I whisper. "Mine ran out." I screw up the bottom of the stick all the way so Dennis can see that it's empty.

"No."

"Why?"

"Because I said so, Polka Dot," Dennis says.

"But it's right there." I point to his glue stick,

which is lying next to scraps of multicolored construction paper. "You didn't even put the cap on. It's going to dry up if you don't let me use it."

"Too bad for you," Dennis says, and he thumps his head on his desk and pretends to nap. I look toward Mrs. Spangle, and she has her own head buried in her bottom desk drawer, digging through her handbag. I peer over the side of Dennis's desk until I can see his face, and he has his eyes closed, ignoring me.

So I reach very slowly around his head, and I lift his glue stick with the very tips of my fingers. Careful not to create any breeze near his Mohawk, I pull my arm back as gently as possible. Success! I pump a silent fist in the air, still clutching Dennis's glue stick, and that's when I see Natalie staring at me.

I pull my other hand across my mouth and then stretch my lips tight, as if I had just zipped them closed, and Natalie nods her head to show she understands that she shouldn't say one thing. Natalie is almost like a real friend ever since she helped me hide Mom's red lipstick on Picture Day. Not like a *best* friend, like Anya is, but she is okay sometimes.

I use Dennis's glue stick to finish putting together my map, and I think about returning it to

his desktop before he notices. But Dennis didn't even let me use his glue stick in the first place, so I don't think he deserves to have it back, at least not yet. I grab the cap from where it is resting just above his Mohawk, place it on the stick, and put it in my own desk. Then I place my empty stick by Dennis's head.

"I like how nicely you've all been working on your maps," Mrs. Spangle says as she stands. "Anything you don't have completed can be wrapped up after recess—you'll all have five minutes to finish. Right now, though, let me see whose group is ready to line up for lunch."

I fold my hands neatly on my desk and sit up super-duper straight, just like Natalie always does. Dennis still has his head resting on his desk, and he is going to ruin it for our whole team. "Psst, Freckle Face." I try to kick him under our desks, but I can't reach. "Wake up."

"I am up," Dennis says, but he still does not lift his head, which means Mrs. Spangle is never going to call us to line up first. I stop sitting super-duper straight, since Dennis is wrecking it for our whole group anyway, and instead, I rustle through my desk until I find my sticker book. Anya and I, and sometimes Natalie, have been collecting stickers and trading them, but mine are some of the prettiest, I think. My favorite kinds of stickers are filled with gel, and when you press them, the gel spreads out and looks glittery. I even traded most of my Rainbow Sparkle stickers for Anya's gel ones, because that is how much I love them.

"Mandy and Dennis, I'll wait," Mrs. Spangle says, so I place my sticker book on my lap and fold my hands again on top of my desk. Dennis places his chin on his hands but still doesn't lift his head.

"Sit up!" I whisper-yell at him, and he does, but not even super-duper straight like he is supposed to.

"Okay, Mandy's group," Mrs. Spangle finally announces. "You can grab your things from the cubbies and get in line." I stand and hold my sticker book up in Anya's direction to make sure she has hers too, and she nods at me. Then I scramble to grab my lunch box and get in line as quickly as I can so I won't be all the way in the back, because Dennis always likes to be the caboose. And there is no way I want Dennis to ruin my appetite today.

"Why'd you steal Dennis's glue stick?" Natalie asks me when we reach our table in the cafeteria.

"I didn't steal it, I took it," I explain.

"Isn't that the same thing?"

I think about this for one second. "No, because if I stole it, I can never give it back, like when

Dennis stole my gummy bears and ate them all. If I took it, I can give it back. I just don't want to yet."

Natalie nods her head like this makes sense, and I am a very good explainer, I think.

I whip my sticker book onto the table and open to the center page, which has all of my favorite gel stickers in a row. "Aren't they beautiful?" I ask.

"They are," Natalie agrees. "My mom said she would take me to the teacher store and look for more stickers this weekend." Teacher stores are one of the best places for getting stickers, because teachers like to buy them almost as much as we do. I have never been to a teacher store, even though I have wanted to go to one my whole entire life. Mom says we do not have to go there because no one in our house is a teacher, but Mom doesn't understand important things like sticker collecting.

"I wonder if Paige has any stickers she would trade," I begin. "Did I tell you she is coming tonight?"

"Only like a thousand times," Anya answers. "I know, you're excited."

"Who's Paige?" Natalie asks.

"Her cousin," Anya answers for me. "Her *favorite* cousin." She drags out the word "favorite" and wiggles her head back and forth as she says it.

"Why is she your favorite?" Natalie asks.

"Because she is fabulous. That is Paige's favorite word, you know—'fabulous.' And that is what she is," I tell her.

"But what makes her so fabulous?" Natalie asks.

"She has wavy hair that looks just like a yellow ocean," I explain. "And she wears boots with little heels that click-clack on the floor. And she has more Rainbow Sparkle stuff than anyone in the universe, and she always draws a heart in her name above the *i*. Oh, and she does not have any brothers or sisters, and that is what I want to have."

"You mean that's what you *don't* want to have?" Natalie asks, and sometimes I wish Natalie would stop listening so much to everything I say, so I sigh an enormous breath at her.

"You know what I mean," I tell her. "Or maybe I would take Paige as my sister. That would be good too."

"Why is she visiting?" Natalie asks.

"Her school is on vacation," I explain. "She will be here for one whole week."

"You're lucky to have a cousin your age," Anya tells me. "All of my cousins are very old. Like, teenagers." And I nod because I agree that I am lucky.

But if I could, I would definitely trade in Timmy and the twins to have Paige as my sister. Then I would be the luckiest girl of all.

CHAPTER 2

Mandy, Not Manda

EVEN THOUGH MOM SAYS THAT GRANDMOM WON'T BE BRINGING Paige over until after eight o'clock, I sit in the living room as soon as we finish dinner, my arms bent on the back of the couch with my chin in my hands, and I look out the window toward the street, waiting.

"A watched pot never boils, Mandy," Dad says as he walks toward the stairs with sheets and pillows stacked high in his arms.

"I'm not watching a pot," I tell him without turning away from the window.

"It's a figure of speech," Dad explains. "It means that waiting for something you really want to happen soon doesn't actually make it happen faster."

"I have been waiting forever to see Paige," I say. "All the way since Christmas." Paige lives many hours away—it takes at least two Rainbow Sparkle chapter books, four word search games, three rounds of "I Spy," and twelve "Are we almost there?" questions to get to my uncle's house. In fact, we have not even been to Paige's house once since the twins were born.

"How about you come help me make Paige's bed?" Dad asks. "It will take your mind off of the waiting."

"Fine," I answer, but only because I do not want Dad snooping around my bedroom without me. There are still a couple bags of gummy bears that he does not know are hidden up there.

I follow him up the stairs and into my room, where Dad has already set up a poufy mattress on the floor next to my bed.

"Wahoo!" I jump onto it like a trampoline and then bounce up and down. "I think I will sleep here."

"You're sleeping in your bed," Dad says. "This air mattress is for Paige. Come on—help me put these sheets on." I pull one corner of the stretchy sheet all the way to one side of the mattress. But just as I am pulling it down around the mattress corner, the doorbell rings.

"Paige is here!" I yell, and I let go of the sheet. I was holding on to it so tightly that it flies back toward Dad like a boomerang.

"Mandy, just a—" Dad calls after me, but I am out the door before he can continue. I run down the stairs as fast as my feet will take me, and I am just about to reach for the knob when the front door swings open and nearly hits me in the head.

"Hey!" I try to yell, but I am pinned between the door and the wall, and all I can hear are everyone's voices but mine.

"Hi, Paige! Hi, Paige! I'm Timmy, remember?"

"Timmy, move back so Paige can get in the door. Come on in, Paige."

"Look at all this grandchild sugar I'm about to get."

"Wahhhhhhh."

"Weeeehhhhh."

Those last two sounds are from the twins, who start wailing of course, because all they know how to do is wail.

"Hey!" I call again, and I push the front door away from me so I'm no longer trapped against the wall. Grandmom, Mom, Timmy, the twins, and most importantly Paige are all gathered in front of me, and Paige looks even more like a princess than I remembered her. Purple heart earrings dangle from her ears, and they match the stack of bangle bracelets stretching up her arm and the purple boots that are click-clacking across the floor. Her hair, which is thick and shiny like golden rainbows, falls down her back like a waterfall.

Paige is absolutely fabulous.

The group walks into the living room, and I run over to hug her around the neck. Before I reach her, Paige pulls one of the twins off of Mom's hip and begins to speak to her. And I stop running immediately, because I try never, ever to touch the twins.

"Shh, don't cry, Samantha. I'm Paige," she coos in the twin's ear. "I'm so happy to meet you."

Timmy hops up and down until Grandmom scoops him into her arms, and he leans way out

until his lips are against Paige's cheek for a wet kiss. Paige giggles at this, and she reaches out with her free hand toward the other twin. She is just about to tickle his arm when I yell "HEY!" for the third time, and I march right over to her. "You didn't say hi to me."

"Amanda, hi," Paige says. "I've just been busy meeting your new brother and sister. They sure are adorable."

"The twins are not adorable," I tell her. "And my name is Mandy now."

"Mandy? Why?" Paige asks, and she still does not even hug me hello.

"Because Mandy has a *y* in it," I explain. "So I like it better."

"You don't look like a Mandy," Paige tells me, which I think is rude. "Plus, I'm used to calling you Amanda."

"But I hate Amanda."

"Then I'll call you Manda," Paige says, and she nods her head once with satisfaction.

"But I don't like—"

"Mandy, I'm waiting for you to give me some sugar," Grandmom interrupts me, leaning down for a kiss, Timmy's arms and legs still wrapped around her like a chimpanzee. When Grandmom is just about to reach my mouth, Timmy slides his face down toward mine in a lick and a split, and he plants a slobbery kiss right on my lips.

"Blech, eww, gross!" I wipe the back of my hands over my lips again and again.

"I give you sugar!" Timmy says, and he looks pretty proud of himself.

"I don't want any preschool sugar," I tell him. "Don't do that again."

"Aww, come on, Manda, that was sweet," Paige says. "Here, Timmy, you can give me some more sugar." She stretches her left cheek toward Timmy's face, and he plants another slobbery kiss right on it.

"Disgusting," I say. "And it's *Mandy*. With a *y*."

"But I think Manda sounds fabulous," Paige tells me. "It's in between Amanda and Mandy."

"That is cute," Mom agrees, and I give her a not-nice look out of the sides of my eyes, but she does not even notice because she is too busy moving the crying twin to her other hip.

Paige has been in my house for less than five minutes, and I am already not sure she is my favorite cousin anymore.

Paige thinks it will be "fun" to help Mom give the twins a bath and put them to bed, and I am absolutely positive that these things are not fun, so I go to my room by myself and wait. Eventually, Timmy and the twins will have to go to bed, and then I will get to have Paige all to myself.

I will show her my new Rainbow Sparkle stuff, and she will tell me all about hers. (I tried to see if Paige brought any of her own Rainbow Sparkle things by peeking in the green sequined duffel bag that Dad placed on Paige's mattress, but I couldn't see inside the bag without taking everything out first, and I did not think Paige would like that much.) She will tell me all about fifth grade, and about what it's like to not have any brothers or sisters, and maybe she will let me try on her click-clack boots. If she does, I will give her some of my gummy bears, because that only seems fair.

Plus, when I have Paige all to myself, I will explain to her that I want to be called Mandy and not Manda, because Manda does not have a curlicue *y* in it, so what is the point? I am sure

Paige will listen to me when those loud twins and Timmy aren't around.

"Mandy, are you in your room?" Dad's voice rings up the stairs.

"Yes," I call back.

"Why are you up there by yourself?" he asks. "Come hang out with us."

"I'm waiting for Paige," I call. "Is she coming up soon?" I hear Dad speaking to someone downstairs, but he is talking too softly for me to understand.

"Okay, she's headed up now," Dad finally calls back, and I hear faint footsteps on the stairs. Seconds later Paige appears in my doorway, and I bounce my behind on my Rainbow Sparkle comforter with happiness.

"It's about time," I tell her. "I have been waiting all night. What color are your pajamas?"

"Um, I forget what I packed," Paige answers. She kneels next to her duffel bag and begins taking her stuff out. "Why do you want to know?"

"Because I will wear whatever color pajamas you are wearing," I explain. "And then we will look just like sisters."

"Ooh, that's fun," Paige says. "I've always wanted a sister."

"Me too," I say.

"You have a sister," Paige points out. "Samantha."

"That does not count," I explain. "I only want an *older* sister, like if you were my sister. You know, I got click-clack shoes too, just like you, only mine are not boots. And I love the handbag you gave me because it has fringe and gemstones so I carry it to—"

"My pajamas are pink," Paige interrupts me, pulling a pink pair of leggings and a huge pink sweatshirt out of her bag. "And they're fabulous." She stands up and changes into them right in front of me, in her underwear and everything, as if she really were my sister. I pop off of my bed and over to my dresser, and I root around in my pajama drawer. Maybe Mom saved some of my old pink nightgowns that I told her to throw out because I do not wear pink things. I dig all the way to the bottom of the drawer, and I find blue and purple and yellow and red and green pajamas, but nothing pink.

"I don't have any pink pajamas." I turn around to face Paige. "Can't you wear something else?"

"These are all I brought," she says. "But don't worry, it's not a big deal."

"Well, what should I wear?" I ask her. "You can pick."

Paige shrugs. "It really doesn't matter to me," and I do not understand why she does not care, because I think it is a very important question. I choose my nightgown with palm trees on it and throw it on top of my bed, then

I step onto Paige's mattress to start bouncing.

"So did you bring any of your Rainbow Sparkle stuff with you?" I ask her.

"I don't really like Rainbow Sparkle anymore," Paige says. "And can you stop bouncing on my bed? It's making me nauseous."

"But it's like a trampoline," I explain, still bouncing. "And why don't you like Rainbow Sparkle anymore? She is my favorite cartoon cat ever."

"I watch other stuff now," Paige says, and she runs her fingers through her hair, turning the waves round and round into loose curls.

"Do you want to play hairdresser?" I ask her. "I will do your hair, and then you can do mine, and then—"

"Nah," Paige interrupts me again. "I don't really like other people touching my hair." And this is terrible news, because I would definitely like to see what Paige's curls feel like. But before I can answer her, Timmy bursts through my bedroom door, even though there is a sign on it with a big X through his name and everything.

"Come on, Paige!" he says, padding into my room in his fire-truck pajamas to grab Paige's hand. Paige reaches out and takes it.

"Oh, so I told Timmy I would sleep in his room tonight," Paige turns over her shoulder to tell me as Timmy drags her toward the door. "Good night, Manda. We can pretend to be twins tomorrow."

Paige and Timmy disappear from my room, and I am left all by myself standing on the mattress, which doesn't even feel much like a trampoline anymore. And I didn't even get to tell Paige that we could never be twins, and not just because I don't like twins.

We could never be twins because Paige has

wavy blond hair and I have straight brown hair, and Paige hates Rainbow Sparkle and I love her, and Paige left me for Timmy, when I was supposed to be her favorite cousin.

And also, I saw Paige's underwear, and it's not even polka dot.

CHAPTER 3

Stinky Toes up Your Nose

I WAKE UP SUPER-DUPER EARLY ON SATURDAY MORNING, and Timmy's bedroom door is closed, which makes me happy, because I do not feel like seeing his or Paige's face yet. I pad down the stairs and into the living room. All of the lights in the house are still off because no one is awake but me, and it is kind of spooky, like a haunted house. I feel a shiver run down my back, and I scurry through the living room quickly, just in case a ghost is chasing me in the dark. When I reach the kitchen, I turn on each and every light so it won't be so scary in here.

"You can't get me now, ghosts," I say out loud, because even though I am not a fraidy cat, I am still a little bit scared of ghosts, if I am being honest. That is because every Halloween, our neighbors, the Packles, turn their entire front porch into a ghost town, and I am never sure where the ghosts go for the rest of the year. Our house is right next door, after all—they might get confused and move in here.

I asked Anya once if she thought there were any ghosts from the Packles' trespassing in my house, and she said probably not, but I like to keep the lights on downstairs just in case. Because everyone knows that ghosts hate bright things.

I slide my feet across the kitchen floor to the refrigerator, and I open the door and peer in. Milk and apples and baby tomatoes are right in front of me, but that is not what I would like for breakfast. I glance all around the refrigerator until I spot them: the chocolate pudding cups hiding on the top shelf. Mom must have moved them yesterday so that Timmy wouldn't be able to reach them anymore, but I am much taller than Timmy, so if I stand on the bottom shelf, I can touch a cup with my fingertips. I step onto the shelf, gripping the edge with my toes, and I stretch my arm as far back as it will go toward the top right corner of the refrigerator. My fingertips tickle the pudding containers, and I scrape my nails against one trying to drag it closer to me.

"And what do you think you're doing?" Dad's voice comes from behind me, and I am so startled that I almost fall backward out of the refrigerator. I hold on to the side of the door to steady myself and then whip around. Dad is standing there holding a twin, and he is smiling in the corners of his mouth, so I am pretty sure I'm not in trouble.

"Getting breakfast," I tell him honestly, and I do not mention that I thought he was a ghost, because that will make me sound like a fraidy cat. I also do not say that I was going to eat pudding for breakfast, because Dad doesn't need to know all of my business.

"If you can wait for everyone else to wake up, I was planning on making pancakes. In fact, if you entertain Cody for a bit, I can get started on them now, and you can have the very first pancake," Dad says.

"The first pancake is the worst," I say, because that is the truth. The first pancake of the batch is always burned and lumpy because the pan is not warmed up yet. Pancake breakfasts are the one and only time that I let Timmy be first at anything, because he does not know the problem with first pancakes yet.

"Fine, the second pancake," Dad says. "What do you say?"

I think about this idea very carefully, because my stomach is grumbly and growly, so I would definitely like to eat pancakes soon. But I also do not want to hold the twin, because the twins are always damp and crying and no fun at all.

"Do I have to hold the twin?" I ask.

"Cody," Dad says. "They do have names, you know, Mandy. And no, I can put him in his chair, but you need to keep him occupied."

"Fine." I nod my head. Dad straps the twin into his baby seat on the kitchen table, and I sit down across from him. I cross my arms and lean all the way back, just to make sure none of the twin's drool can reach me.

"Here is a secret," I say. "The first pancake of

the batch is always the worst. It is burned and it is lumpy and it is best to make Timmy eat it. Also, the best kinds of gummy bears are the red ones, but if you ever touch my gummy bears, you will be in major trouble. And the best bite of a pizza slice is the first one, right on the tip of the triangle, because it has the most cheese, so you should always give those bites to me. Oh, and the best color is periwinkle." The twin stares back at me as I tell him all of these important things, and he is being quiet for once. This twin has brown eyes that look a little bit like mine and tufts of brown hair growing out of his head.

He might not be too bad-looking if he weren't so damp all the time.

"I am out of things to say." I turn around in my seat and face Dad, and he has pulled all of the ingredients to make pancakes out onto the counter.

"I find that hard to believe," Dad tells me. "Pretend you're talking to Anya. Cody just likes the sound of your voice."

I squish my eyebrows together and think about what I would say to Anya, and then I begin. "Paige is a big traitor. She slept in Timmy's room instead of mine, and that should not be allowed. Because she is supposed to be *my* favorite cousin."

"Is that true?" Dad interrupts my conversation with the twin, and I nod my head.

"She did not even lie down for one second on the bouncy mattress," I tell him.

"I bet she was just trying to be fair to Timmy," Dad says. "I'm sure she'll sleep in your room tonight."

"I do not even want her to," I say. "I want Anya to sleep over instead." And I pause for a moment because that is the best idea I have ever had. "Can Anya come over?"

"You'll have to ask your mother," Dad says. "But I don't think you should have a sleepover. There are already enough people in this house this weekend. Maybe Anya can come just for a playdate." Dad pours the first ladle of pancake batter into the frying pan, and it begins to wheeze and hiss.

And I almost hope Paige wakes up soon, because I know just the pancake that I will offer her for breakfast.

Mom says it is okay for Anya to come over and play, so I call her as soon as it is late enough and ask her if she would like to. Her mom drops her off at my house right after breakfast, and I run out the front door to greet her before she is all the way to our stoop.

"Let's go, let's go, hurry!" I grab her by the wrist and pull her into my house and up the stairs.

"Where are we going so fast?" Anya asks, but I do not answer her until we are all the way in my room with the door closed.

"We are playing by ourselves," I explain to her. "No Timmy, no twins, and no Paige."

"I thought you loved Paige," Anya says.

"Not anymore," I say. "She slept in Timmy's room last night instead of mine, and then she talked to the twins all during breakfast, and she didn't even say thank you when I gave her the first pancake."

"Blech, but the first pancake is the worst," Anya says, and this is why she is my favorite person in the world, at least most of the time: because Anya understands all of the rules about pancakes and pizza and gummy bears.

"That is why I gave it to her," I say. "Because she is the worst. But she did not even notice because she was too busy playing This Little Piggy on the twins' feet. And everyone knows the twins' feet are gross."

"All feet are gross," Anya agrees. "Unless you have painted toenails, then they're okay." And my eyes grow wide then, because Anya has given me another great idea.

"We should paint our nails," I tell her. "And paint them all the same color, like we are sisters."

Anya nods her head up and down ferociously until her wispy curls are almost covering her eyes. Anya's hair is a little bit wavy too, but it has more curls than Paige's, and because I like Anya better than Paige right now, I think hers is prettier.

I kneel on the floor and then place my entire head under my bed until I find what I'm looking for: three bottles of nail polish that Mom doesn't know are missing from her bathroom. I line the bottles up in front of Anya.

"You pick the color," I say, and Anya looks at them each very carefully.

"This one." She points to a dark purple color that looks almost like a plum, and I am so glad that she did not pick the pink polish that I could hug her.

"That's what I would have picked too," I tell her. "Because it is the closest one to periwinkle. Do you want to do my feet, and I'll paint yours?"

"Definitely," Anya says, and she pulls off her shoes and socks and spreads her ten toes out in front of me.

"One second." I leap up from the floor and pull my entire comforter off of my bed. I toss it on top of the bouncy mattress in a heap, and then I pull my gummy bear bag out from under my pillow. "This mattress will help make a good Magic Mountain Wonderland."

I sit on the side of the mountain, and Anya

scoots over toward the mattress and then throws her behind right in the middle of the comforter. The whole heap collapses, and it doesn't really look like a mountain anymore, but Anya and I are giggling too much about it to care. She lifts her right foot into my face so that her big toe is under my nostrils.

"I am ready for my beauty treatment," she says.

"Then get your stinky toes out of my nose," I say, batting at her foot like it is a fly, which makes Anya laugh more.

"Hey, that rhymed," Anya tells me. "Stinky toes up your nose, stinky toes up your nose." And now we are laughing so loudly that we don't even hear when my bedroom door opens and Paige waltzes in, without knocking or anything.

"Hi." She walks right up to Anya. "I'm Manda's cousin, Paige."

Anya glances at me with a question in her eyes.

"I'm Anya, *Mandy's* best friend," Anya answers her, and she says the *y* part of my name super-duper loud.

"What are you two up to?" Paige asks.

"Doing our nails," Anya answers her. "We're painting all of our finger and toenails the same color—all forty of them. Sister nails."

"Ooh, can I join you?" Paige asks, and she starts to sit down on top of Magic Mountain Wonderland. Anya looks at me out of the corner of her eye, waiting for me to answer.

"We do not have enough polish," I tell her. "You better go in Timmy's room and play with him." I unscrew the bottle of purple polish and reach out for Anya's foot. "Stinky toe, please." Anya places her foot on my knee, and I paint careful strokes of purple up and down on her big toe. Without saying another word, Paige walks out of my bedroom and closes the door behind her.

"That might have been kind of mean," Anya whispers to me.

"*She's* kind of mean," I say. "If she weren't, she would have slept in my room last night and not Timmy's. And she would know my name is Mandy. With a *y*. Not a stupid *a*."

"Right," Anya agrees, and I concentrate very hard on painting all the rest of her toenails perfectly, without spilling one drop.

And when Anya begins to paint my own nails, I have never been more sure that it is much more important to have a best friend than it is to have a favorite cousin. Because your best friend will never, ever choose your dumb brothers and sisters over you.

CHAPTER 4

A Not-Eggcellent Plan

"MANDY," I HEAR MOM CALLING FROM THE BOTTOM OF THE stairs. "Come down here for a second, please." I groan like a dinosaur at Anya and rise slowly to my feet.

"Do you think Paige tattletaled on us?" she asks, and she sounds a little panicky.

"I don't know," I tell her. "But you will not get in trouble with my mom because she only likes to punish me."

"Mandy!" Mom calls again, and I stomp my feet over to my bedroom door and open it.

"What?" I call without leaving my room.

"Come down here, please." I turn around and roll my eyes all the way to the ceiling so Anya can see, and then I shuffle my feet over to the top of the stairs.

"What?" I stare down the steps at Mom like I am a giant and she is an ant, and she motions for me to walk down them. I lean my right arm hard against the banister and try to slide my way down so that my feet barely have to touch the steps, because I do not want to mess up my toenails on the carpet.

"I thought I asked you not to play on the stairs," Mom says when I finally reach her.

"My nails are wet," I explain.

"Let me see." I hold out my left arm and lift my right leg onto the banister so Mom can examine them. It is a pretty high stretch, and I am very flexible, I think.

"They look great," Mom says, and she is being awfully nice for someone Paige tattletaled to about me. "Where'd you get that polish?"

I feel my eyes grow into wide pancakes then, because I forgot about that little detail.

Mom smiles. "Don't worry about it, I never liked that color anyway," she says. "Keep it. But next time, ask me first, please."

"Okay." I pull my ankle off the banister carefully so that I don't fall backward.

"You're welcome," Mom prompts me.

"Thank you," I say. "Why did you call me?"

"Anya has to leave in a little bit," Mom says. "Grandmom is coming over soon, and we want to have a family afternoon with Paige. I thought you'd want to tell Anya yourself."

"Can I go to Anya's house instead?" I ask.

"No, you're staying here with us," Mom says. "Either Anya can call her parents to pick her up or

Dad will drive her home. Have her find out what they want to do."

"'Kay," I answer. "But I wish Anya could stay."

"I know, but you get to see her almost every day all year," Mom says. "You only get to visit with Paige this week. You better enjoy it."

I turn on my heel and walk quietly up the stairs without answering Mom, because a whole week left with Paige does not seem very enjoyable at all.

Grandmom turns into our driveway just as Anya's mom's car pulls away, and I watch as Timmy and Paige, a twin dangling off both of her hips, run to the front door to greet her. I sit on the armchair in the living room with my legs crisscrossed into a pretzel, and I do not budge.

Paige and I have not said one word to each other since she was in my room, and I am not going to speak first. But at least she didn't tattletale to Mom about Anya and me not letting her paint nails with us—that is something, I guess.

When Grandmom enters, the four of them almost tackle her, but I stay in the chair, annoyed. "I love having so many of my grandchildren in one place," Grandmom says, and she plants a kiss on each of them, one right after another, taking one of the twins from Paige. "Mandy, where's my sugar?"

"You can get it over here," I say, and I still don't move off of the chair.

"Mandy, get up and give your grandmother a kiss." Mom enters the living room and takes the other twin from Paige. I uncross my legs slowly and shuffle toward Grandmom, who lifts my chin in her hands and kisses me on the lips.

"That's better," Grandmom says.

"Me again!" Timmy insists, and Grandmom gives him another kiss, which I think is way too many. Only grandmoms would want to kiss a preschooler that much.

"Yuck," I say quietly, but Grandmom hears me anyway.

"How could I resist five of the sweetest grandchildren in the world?" she asks.

"Who's the sweetest?" Paige asks her, and I am not positive, but I am pretty sure she glances at me when she says this, so I give her my "You are driving me bananas" face.

"You're all sweet in your own way," Grandmom answers. "How was your slumber party last night?" She looks back and forth from me to Paige.

"Paige slept with Timmy," I answer.

"Only for last night," she pipes up. "I told you I would sleep in your room tonight. If you still want me to."

I shrug my shoulders, because Mom and Grandmom are watching me, so I cannot tell Paige no.

"Well, maybe you two can make yourselves a midnight snack for tonight," Grandmom says, and she digs in her enormous pocketbook until she finds what she's looking for. "Because I got a little something for you to work on together while Paige is in town." She holds out a book, and the cover is plastered in pictures of cupcakes and brownies and macaroni and cheese.

"Yum!" Timmy calls when he sees it.

"Ooh, a kids' cookbook," Paige reads the title. "Thanks, Grandmom!"

"I have a little challenge for you two," Grandmom continues. "You know that carnival that is in town this week at the Whisk Avenue parking lot? If you two learn to cook—"

"The carnival?" I interrupt her, and my voice sounds like more of a squeak than I would have liked. "I've wanted to go to the carnival my whole entire life!" The carnival comes to our town every single year, and every single year Mom says we are going to go, and then we don't.

At least, every year since Timmy was born. We used to go to the carnival when I was still an only child like Paige. Before Timmy and the twins ruined everything.

"I'm glad you're so enthusiastic about it," Grandmom says. "So as I was saying, if you two learn to cook five dishes with no grown-ups, except to help with the oven and anything with knives, I thought I'd take you there next Friday, when you have off from school, Mandy, and before Paige leaves. What do you say?"

"Yes, I think that's great!" Paige answers immediately, and she grabs the cookbook from Grandmom before I can say one word. "Come on, Manda, let's get started."

"It's MANDY," I say, yelling the Y part extra loud. "It is not hard to remember."

"Whatever," Paige mumbles under her breath as she continues to the kitchen without even turning around, so I do not follow her.

"What do you say, Mandy?" Grandmom asks. "Wouldn't you like to go to the carnival too?"

"Yes," I answer honestly. "But I don't want to cook with her." And I say "her" like I am talking about the twins' snot.

"Listen to me," Mom begins. "Paige is a guest in our house this week. It's your job to make her feel welcome. Got it?"

"But she keeps calling me Manda instead of Mandy," I tell her. "Plus, she slept in Timmy's room last night, after she was supposed to sleep in mine."

"Then talk to her about it. Nicely," Mom says. "Paige is a smart girl. I'm sure she'll understand. Now, shoo. Get cooking if you want to go to the carnival with Grandmom on Friday." Mom points in the direction of the kitchen, and I slump my shoulders and look at the nail polish on my toes, but I do not move my feet one inch.

"Mandy, I'd really like to take you and Paige to the carnival, but this requires a little cooperation on your part," Grandmom says. "What do you say?"

And I say nothing, but I shuffle into the kitchen to join Paige at the counter.

"I can't mess up my nails," I tell her as a greeting. "So you have to do all the messy parts."

"We're going to make egg salad," Paige says. "There are a lot of eggs and mayonnaise in the refrigerator, so we'll have enough."

"I don't like egg salad," I say, because that is the truth. Egg salad is slimy and goopy and tastes like wet rubber. I have not eaten egg salad since first grade, when Mom packed me an egg salad sandwich instead of peanut butter and jelly, and I left the whole sandwich in my lunch box unwrapped. Mom was not too happy about this, because it made a gigantic mess, but at least she has not made me eat the stuff again.

"I love it," Paige says. "Get the eggs out of the refrigerator."

"I just told you, I don't like egg salad," I repeat. "I want to make something else."

"Well, I want to make this," Paige says, staring down her nose at me, and I think she might just be the bossiest person in the world, even bossier than Natalie.

"I am not making egg salad," I say. "If you want to make it, you can do it by yourself."

"Fine," Paige says, and she pushes right past me toward the refrigerator. "I'll go by myself to the carnival with Grandmom, then, too."

"Oh, no, you won't," I say. "Grandmom likes me better than you anyway."

"No, she doesn't," Paige says. "She likes me the best, because I'm the oldest. Everyone always likes the oldest best."

"*I'm* the oldest," I say. "Timmy and the twins are much younger than me."

"But I'm the oldest *grandchild*. You're just the oldest in the Berr house. You weren't Grandmom's first granddaughter. I was."

I scramble in my brain to think of what to say to this, but Grandmom walks into the kitchen before I can let out one peep.

"How are we doing in here?" she asks us.

"Who's your favorite grandchild?" I ask her.

"What?"

"Who is your favorite grandchild?" I repeat, and I say each word slowly to make sure Grandmom understands.

"I don't have a favorite," Grandmom answers. "I love all of my grandchildren the same." And I think this is a lie, because everyone has a favorite everything. "Now, how are we doing with the cooking?"

"I'm making egg salad," Paige says.

"Sounds yummy," Grandmom says. "Mandy, are you helping?"

"I hate egg salad," I answer.

"Well, I bet if you help Paige with this recipe, you'll get to pick the dish next time. Right, Paige?" Grandmom prompts.

"Right," Paige answers, but I am absolutely positive that if Grandmom weren't standing next to her, she would never have agreed. "So can you get the eggs, please?" Paige asks me this in her sweetest voice, and I know it is only because Grandmom is listening.

I sigh an enormous breath but pad over to the refrigerator, pull out the carton of eggs, and place it on the counter next to Paige. And I really wish my parents had taken me to the carnival just once in the past three years so that I wouldn't want to go so badly now. Because if I have to spend much more time with Paige, I am pretty sure I am going to throw up egg salad all over the kitchen.

CHAPTER 5

Pizza Pops

I WAKE UP SUNDAY MORNING WITH GRUMBLIES IN MY STOMACH again, because all we had to eat for dinner was dumb egg salad. I told everybody over and over that I do not like egg salad, and Mom said that if I really wanted to eat something else, I had to cook it myself. But there was no way I was going to cook anything else with bossy Paige around, yammering over my shoulder the whole time. No way! So I went to bed without even eating a pudding cup, which is very unfair.

Paige slept in Timmy's room again, because I told her that she smelled like egg salad. But I am kind of glad she is there now, because I don't like Paige the way I used to. I liked Paige when she had Rainbow Sparkle stuff and she let me try on her click-clack boots and she told me that I was her favorite cousin. This Paige who is visiting now is no fun at all.

I pull my Rainbow Sparkle comforter off of me and stretch down toward my feet, and I smile when I see the purple polish on my toenails. I bounce out of bed and hop up and down on the trampoline mattress that Paige is supposed to be sleeping on. My stomach grumblies get very angry then and let out a big growl, so I decide I better go find them something to eat.

I open my bedroom door as quietly as I can and pad down the stairs, and I do not trip once even though there are no lights on and it's still dark outside. I cannot risk turning on the hall-way lights because I do not want anyone else to wake up yet, especially not Timmy and Paige. I run through the living room and into the kitchen and turn on every light I can find, just like I did yesterday morning. When the whole downstairs is bright, I let out a big gust of air, realizing that I had been holding my breath until I knew there were no ghosts in the house. All of these lights will keep me safe now, I think.

The clock on the microwave reads 5:24. That is super-duper early, even for the twins, and I skip around the counter a few times at the thought of having so much time by myself. I open the refrigerator door, but all I see right in front of me is Paige's egg salad, and there is no way I am eat-ing that for breakfast. I keep the refrigerator open just to have some extra light on in case a ghost comes around, and I pull the kids' cookbook off of the counter. I flip through the pages looking at the pictures, and then my eyes land on it: pizza. I can make my very own pizza and eat all of the corner bites by myself, and no one can say one word about it! Grandmom definitely should have mentioned this page when she gave us the book.

I place an empty bowl in the middle of the cookbook to keep it open to the pizza page, and I read the list of ingredients: *tortillas, tomato sauce, mozzarella cheese, pepperoni, broccoli, onions, and mushrooms.*

I do not like broccoli, onions, or mushrooms, so I take those off of the list right away. I look around in the refrigerator, peering on all of the shelves and in each of the drawers. There is a package of bright orange cheddar cheese slices in one drawer, but nothing that says "mozzarella." I place the cheddar cheese on the counter, and I read the list of ingredients again: *tortillas, tomato sauce, pepperoni.*

Hmm.

I look all around the refrigerator again, but I do not see any of these things. I place the bag of white bread next to the cheddar cheese, and then I pull the jumbo-size bottle of ketchup out of the refrigerator door. Ketchup is much better than tomato sauce anyway, I think. Because ketchup is best friends with French fries, so it has very good taste in friends.

The only thing missing now is the pepperoni, and I study the picture of the pizza with the small circles of pepperoni slices sprinkling the top. I look in the pantry, and the only round things I see are these salty crackers that Mom sometimes gives us as a snack with the cheddar cheese. This means that the crackers taste good with the cheese—plus, they are round, so they will be a good pepperoni substitute.

I roll up the sleeves of my pajamas and get to

work. But even if I stand all the way on my tippy toes, it is still hard for me to reach everything on the counter. I walk into the toy room and turn the light on, then I pick up one of the chairs from the stupid kiddie table where Mom and Dad like to make me eat with Timmy. I carry it into the kitchen and place it next to the counter, and I step on top of it. Now I am the perfect height.

I undo the twisty tie on the bread bag and place a slice on the counter in front of me. I look back at the recipe· *Spread tomato sauce on top of the tortilla.* I lift the gigantic bottle of ketchup, turn it upside down, and flip open the cap. An enormous stream of ketchup shoots out of the bottle, onto the slice of bread, and onto the counter, too, and I quickly flip the bottle back over and hop off of the chair to get a spoon. I then spread the ketchup all over the slice of bread with the back of the spoon, and I look like a real chef now, I think.

Top with cheese. Assemble pepperoni slices and vegetables.

I make a face at the word "vegetables," and I pull a slice of cheddar cheese out of the package. It covers most of the bread slice, but not all of it, and cheese is the best part of pizza anyway, so I take another slice out of the package. Then I place four crackers on top of the cheese so that they look like pepperoni.

Bake at 350, the recipe says, and since I do not know how to turn on the oven without a grown-up, I lift up the corners of my pizza, carry it carefully over to the microwave, open the door, and place it inside. Then I press 3 and 5 on the microwave's number pad, followed by the ON button. I watch my pizza start to turn around and around inside, and I lick my lips as my stomach grumblies start to complain again.

While I wait, I decide to make myself another

pizza, because I am very, very hungry. The micro-wave whirls and hums as I assemble another ketchup-smothered bread slice, topping the whole thing with two slices of cheese again. I perfectly place the crackers into position, lift up the pizza, and begin to step off of the chair to bring it to the microwave.

Pop!

Pop! Pop! Pop!

Hisssssssssss.

POP!

I slip the rest of the way off of the chair and accidentally throw the second pizza over my head. The chair topples onto its side with a crash, and I hit the floor with a thud. The pizza splats back onto the counter, while the popping sound continues from across the kitchen. I start crawling on my hands and knees as fast as I can toward the living room, trying to hide from the ghost that I am sure has snuck into my house, even though all of the lights are on and everything. My knees scrape against the floor, but I duck down as far as I can and scramble out of the kitchen.

I glance over my shoulder to make sure a ghost isn't following me, and then I slam right into it: the ghost himself.

"Arghhhhhh!" I scream at the top of my lungs, and I try to back away from the ghost, scooting across the floor on my bottom.

"Mandy, Mandy, it's me." Dad stoops down so his face is next to mine, but he is still hard to see in the darkness of the living room. "What is going on in there?"

"I thought you were a ghost!" I tell him.

"What is that sound in the kitchen?" Dad steps over me to investigate, but my heart is beating so hard that I am sure it is going to have a fight with my stomach grumblies. I hear a beeping sound, and then the whirl of the microwave stops. One last *pop* echoes across the room.

"Mandy, what—how—why—I can't—" Dad stutters, and I see him looking all around the kitchen. He opens the door of the microwave, and even from the floor, I can see it: my beautiful pizza, exploded. Orange and red cover the entire inside of the microwave, like the ugly finger paintings Timmy makes in preschool.

"I was hungry," I tell Dad, finally lifting myself onto my feet. "And I wanted pizza. Not dumb egg salad."

"Does this look like pizza to you?" Dad points in the microwave and then to my second pizza, which is lying upside down on the counter, the crackers broken and the ketchup running down the side like blood. "And how long did you set this for?"

"I pressed three and five," I answer.

"Thirty-five *minutes*?" he exclaims.

"That's what it said in the cookbook," I explain. "'Bake at 350,' but I knew I was not allowed to touch the oven, because I am very good at following that rule, so I put it in the microwave instead."

"It's not even six a.m. yet," Dad says with a sigh. "How could you possibly have made such a mess before six a.m.? Really, even for you, Mandy, this is a record." He looks around the kitchen one more time, like he is still a little bit asleep. "Here's what we're going to do: You clean up this whole catastrophe you have going on in here, and if the kitchen looks pristine—even better than when you entered it—by the time everyone else wakes up, I won't have to take away Rainbow Sparkle's TV show this week."

I slump my shoulders and push my lips together into a pout, but I do not disagree. "Let me know when you're ready for me to examine your work. I'll be waiting on the couch," Dad says, padding out of the kitchen and into the living room, shutting off one of the kitchen lights on his way. "And why does it look like Grand Central Station in here? You're wasting electricity." I watch him walk to the couch, and while his back is turned, I skedaddle to the light switch and flip it back on. Even if it was my pizza and not a ghost popping and hissing at me, you can still never be too careful when it comes to keeping them away.

I walk over to the paper towel holder and begin to unwind a huge glob, but then my stomach growls at me—the grumblies even angrier than they were before. I place the paper towels back on the counter, lift the chair off the ground, step on top of it, and then make myself one more pizza slice, this time with no crackers. Without placing it in the microwave, I take a gigantic bite out of my white bread, cheddar cheese, and ketchup pizza.

And no matter what anyone else says, I know it is the best pizza I have ever had.

CHAPTER 6

No Bossing My Brother

I HAVE NEVER BEEN HAPPIER TO SEE MY CLASSROOM THAN I am on Monday morning. I am so glad to get away from Paige and Timmy and the twins and exploding pizzas and trespassing ghosts that the minute I see Mrs. Spangle, I throw my arms around her waist and squeeze her.

"What's this for?" she asks, but she squeezes my shoulders right back.

"I am happy to see you," I tell her.

"Well, that's a great attitude for a Monday,"

Mrs. Spangle replies. "Thanks for the boost, Mandy."

I trot off into the cubbies, and Anya is standing in front of mine. I throw my arms around her neck from the back, and I think I tackle her a little bit.

"You're choking me!" she calls, but she is laughing about it, so I know I am not really hurting her. I release her, and she spins around.

"How's Paige?" she asks.

"Ugh," I answer. "Bossy. Annoying. I would like her to go home now."

"Who?" Natalie pipes up from behind me, and I do not even mind that she is interrupting, even though I usually do not like people to butt in on my beeswax.

"Paige, my cousin," I answer.

"I thought you loved her," Natalie says as she takes off her jacket.

I shake my head back and forth ferociously. "Not anymore."

"Why?" Natalie asks.

"Because I do not," I tell her. "But I don't want to talk about her anymore. I want to talk about the stickers you bought at the teacher store."

"I didn't get to go," Natalie says, and she looks pretty sad about it. "My mom said maybe this week."

Before I can agree with Natalie that this is a tragedy, Dennis steps right in between us, which I think is rude.

"I know that you took my glue stick," he says to me.

"You don't know anything, Freckle Face," I tell him.

Dennis puts his nose very close to mine, so close that I can smell the hair gel in his Mohawk, and I think he uses way too much.

"Just wait until you see what I glue things with

now, Polka Dot," Dennis whispers, and he walks out of the cubbies before I can answer.

"What'd he say?" Anya asks.

"Nothing," I say. "I'll take care of him."

But thanks to Dennis, I am much less excited to be back at school than I was five minutes ago.

Dennis is on his best behavior for the rest of the day, which I think is suspicious. He does not take any of my things or call me any name-calls or bother me one bit. In fact, by the end of the day, Mrs. Spangle announces that Dennis can pick a prize from her treasure box for not getting his initials on the board all day, and he skips off happily to claim his reward.

And when he smiles at me extra wide on his way back to our group, I then know for sure that he is up to something.

"What'd you pick?" I ask.

"None of your business," Dennis answers, and he sticks his prize in his desk before I can see.

"Come on, show me," I say.

"I said, none of your business, Polka Dot," Dennis repeats, and I am almost happy to hear him call me "Polka Dot," because at least he is acting normal again.

I reach into my own desk to pull out my sticker book, just so I have something nice to look at as we pack to go home. I move my fingers around the left side of my desk where the book usually is, but I do not feel it. I pull out all of the folders and books and papers that are on that side and place them on my lap, then I look in between each of them one by one. Nothing.

Just as I am about to reach inside again and remove everything on the right side of my desk, I catch Dennis watching me.

Not just watching me—laughing at me.

"Looking for something?" he asks.

"You took it," I say.

"I have no idea what you're talking about," Dennis responds, so I shoot my hand in the air and wave it in Mrs. Spangle's direction.

"I wouldn't do that if I were you," Dennis says. "Unless you want to talk about what you did with my glue stick."

I remove my hand from the air slowly and stare at Dennis. "Give it back," I say.

Dennis shrugs. "I said, I don't know what you're talking about."

I slam my palms onto the top of my desk, and they make a louder noise than I was expecting. Mrs. Spangle whips around and looks at me.

"Excuse me," she says with a warning in her voice. "Mandy and Dennis, your group was having such a good day today. Don't tell me that's going to change now."

I remove my hands from my desk and place all of my belongings back inside of it, but I keep my eyes on Dennis the whole time. Then, when I'm sure Mrs. Spangle isn't watching, I rock my chair back on two legs to get closer to Anya.

"Dennis stole my sticker book," I whisper in her ear, and Anya turns her head around and stares at me with wide pancake eyes.

"Are you sure?" she asks, and I nod my head.

"Don't worry," she says. "We'll get it back tomorrow."

I bring my chair back down to four legs carefully so that Mrs. Spangle doesn't hear, and I glare through narrow eyes at Dennis until the bell rings.

I bang in the front door after school, and I am greeted by the sound of the twins wailing. This is not a surprise, because all the twins do is wail.

The crying sound is coming from the twins'

room, so I decide to stay far away from there as I walk toward the kitchen for a snack. Paige is standing behind the counter, one of Mom's aprons draped around her neck and covering the front of her clothes. White powder is sprinkled over most of the countertop, though I cannot tell from where I am if it is flour or sugar or salt. But I am pretty sure that if I were the one who was making such a mess in the kitchen, I would be in pretty big trouble about it.

I walk toward the pantry without opening my mouth, and then I hear Paige say, "Hand me the spatula."

"No!" I answer instantly, whirling around to face her. "I am not—" But Paige is not even looking at me; she's looking down to the ground. And then I see a plastic spatula being raised toward her hand.

"I wasn't talking to you," Paige says without

glancing at me. "I was talking to Timmy." And Timmy comes crawling out from behind the counter then, and he does not look very happy about it either.

"We cooking," he tells me.

"You are supposed to be cooking with me," I tell Paige. "Not Timmy. Grandmom said so."

"You were at school," Paige answers.

"I *have* to go to school."

Paige shrugs. "That's not my problem. *I* am on vacation this week."

"In *my* house," I point out.

"You didn't want to cook with me anyway," Paige says, and I think about this for one second, because that is the truth. But that still does not give Paige the right to cook without me.

"Timmy, stand up, you're in my way," Paige continues before I can answer her. "And wash your hands so you can help me with this."

"Stop bossing him around," I tell her. "You are not the boss of everybody."

"I'm not bossing him around," Paige says. "We're working together."

"No, you're being bossy," I say. "Timmy, isn't she being bossy?"

"Yep!" Timmy answers, and I almost like Timmy right then, except not too much.

"Told you so," I say to Paige, and she squints her eyes at me in a not-nice way.

"Why don't you just leave us alone? We were having a nice time until you came home," she says to me.

"Timmy, were you having a nice time?" I ask.

"No!" Timmy answers, and he stands up and walks over to me, like I am his favorite person in the room instead of Paige.

"Come on," I say. "You don't have to listen to her anymore." I march out of the kitchen, and

Timmy follows behind me, stomping his feet on the ground almost as loudly as I do.

"Now *you're* bossing him around," Paige calls after me.

"I am allowed, because he is my brother!" I yell back. "Not yours!"

Mom walks toward us with one twin drooling on her shoulder. "Everything okay out here?" she asks.

"It is now," I say, and Timmy trails me up the stairs, leaving Paige all by herself in the kitchen.

Which is just the way we both like it.

CHAPTER 7

Mattress Removal

WHEN I REACH MY ROOM, I MARCH INSIDE AND STRAIGHT over to the bouncy mattress on the floor. Timmy stands watching me from the doorway, not sure whether he should step inside.

"Well, are you going to help me?" I ask, and I lift up two corners of the mattress, which is heavier than it should be for something that is so good at being a trampoline. Timmy runs in my room and flops on top of the mattress, which throws him a couple of inches in the air.

And this is why it is very difficult to get help from a preschooler.

"You're making it even heavier!" I tell him, and he scrambles onto his feet again.

"What you doing, Mandy?"

"I am taking this dumb mattress out of my room because I do not want Paige to think she is allowed to sleep in here anymore," I say. "Now try to lift up one of the other corners for me."

Timmy walks to the other end of the mattress and follows my directions, but the mattress doesn't budge.

"Humph." I frown. "Maybe we can kick it out." I stand on the side of the mattress farthest from the door and lift my right foot all the way back to kick it, just like I am about to kick a soccer ball.

"You break toes," Timmy says, reminding me of the time that I kicked my foot into the bottom of the kitchen counter and accidentally broke my longest toe.

"Good point," I tell him. "Plus, I might chip my toenail polish. Maybe we have to drag it." I step back over the mattress to the other side, and it throws me around like it is a moon bounce. I bend down toward the corner closest to the door, wrap both of my hands around it, and try to move it along the floor.

And it moves!

"I am a genius," I tell Timmy. "You push from that side." So I pull on my side of the mattress, and Timmy pushes on his, until we have moved the entire thing out of my room and into the hallway. Timmy looks up at me then, waiting for me to decide what to do, and I am glad he thinks that I am the real boss of this house.

"Do you want it in your room?" I ask him, and he shakes his head back and forth ferociously.

"Then we'll just leave it here," I say. "She can sleep in the hallway."

Timmy nods his head in agreement, and I like that he is on my side.

"Good teamwork," I say, and I reach out my hand for Timmy to shake, just like Mrs. Spangle makes us do after we finish a game of kickball. Timmy slaps my hand like a high five instead, but I do not even mind too much.

Because at least Timmy agrees with me that Paige deserves to sleep in the hallway.

Later that afternoon, when I am lying on my bed reading a Rainbow Sparkle book and minding my own beeswax, I hear footsteps coming up the stairs. They pause outside of my bedroom, right near where Timmy and I left the bouncy mattress. A couple of seconds later Paige appears in my doorway.

"Why is my bed in the hallway?" she asks.

"Because I don't want it in my room," I tell her.

"So where am I supposed to sleep?"

I shrug my shoulders. "Wherever you want. But not in my room." I turn back to my Rainbow Sparkle book, signaling that it is time for her to go. She takes the hint and leaves my doorway, and I go back to reading in peace.

"Amanda. Down here. Now," Mom calls from the bottom of the stairs, and I groan like a dinosaur and slide off the top of my bed like a snake. I walk out of my room and down the stairs as slowly as I can, and that's when I see it: Mom and Paige sitting on the living room couch, Mom's arm around Paige's shoulder.

And Paige is crying.

"You've made Paige very upset," Mom says. "Care to explain yourself?" And I am too busy thinking about how I have never made an older kid cry before to come up with a good answer to Mom's question.

"I'm waiting," Mom says, interrupting my thoughts.

"I moved her mattress," I finally answer.

"To where?"

"The hallway."

"Why?"

"Because I do not want her to sleep in my room."

"You have to learn to share your space and your things."

I feel my eyes grow into enormous pancakes then, because Mom is not understanding me. "I *was* sharing," I say. "Paige is the one who never has to share anything because she doesn't have any brothers or sisters. So she thinks she is the boss of everybody, and that is a lie."

"I think you owe Paige an apology. A big one," Mom tells me.

"Why? She is the one who is mean to me."

"I'm waiting, Amanda."

"Plus, she only calls me Manda even though I keep telling her my name is Mandy."

"I'm going to count to three," Mom begins.

"Timmy should have to apologize too. He helped me move the mattress."

"I'll speak with Timmy next. This is about you. One . . ."

I sigh a huge sigh then and look at Paige's face, which is red and splotchy around her eyes from crying.

"I'm sorry I moved your bed," I say, then I look back to Mom. "Am I done?"

"Paige was already going to have a sleepover at Grandmom's tonight anyway," Mom answers me. "But when she is back, I expect the two of you to work on getting along. You are family. You're going to fight sometimes, of course, but it's more important that you are there for each other."

I do not say one thing about this, and neither does Paige. And when Grandmom comes to pick her up, she does not even call me to the door to give her some sugar. Instead, she takes Paige to her car all by herself for the whole night, because maybe Paige really is her favorite grandchild.

I walk right past Mrs. Spangle and into my classroom the next morning, and she calls after me, "Boy, not even a hello this morning after a hug yesterday. What did I do to deserve this?" I scurry back over to her and give her a hug like I mean it, and for a minute I think about telling her about Dennis and my sticker book. But if I do, then Dennis will definitely tattletale on me about the glue stick, and I do not feel like being in trouble at school, too, since I am already in trouble at home for moving Paige's bed.

I deposit my things in my cubby and walk over to my seat. Dennis is already sitting at our group, but he has his face buried inside of his desk, looking for something, and all I can see is his Mohawk.

"Remember, your seatwork sheets are at the front of the room. Cut out the squares that show the scenes from the story we read yesterday, and then glue them in the correct sequence onto the construction paper. Who can remind me what 'sequence' is?"

I shoot my hand in the air, but Mrs. Spangle calls on Natalie.

"The order things happened in the story," Natalie answers.

"Excellent," Mrs. Spangle says. "When you finish gluing your story sequences, you can color in the pictures on each square." I pick up my sheets from the front of the room and return to my desk, and I am shocked to see that Dennis already has his squares cut out and placed on the construction paper, ready to be glued, because Dennis does not usually do any work quickly, if he even does it at all.

I remove my scissors from my desk and begin cutting the squares apart, and I concentrate very hard on staying on the dotted lines. Then I study each square carefully until I decide in which order they should be glued on the construction paper. It is only when I am reaching in my desk for Dennis's glue stick that I see it, and before I can bite my tongue to stop myself, I scream.

And I scream pretty loud, if I am being honest. Because I am an excellent screamer.

Anya and Mrs. Spangle both rush over to my group, and that's when they see it too: Dennis is not using a glue stick or liquid glue or paste or anything he is supposed to in order to glue his squares to the construction paper. Instead, he is using MY STICKERS. From my sticker book! He is using the stickers like tape to hold the squares onto the paper, and even worse, he is using the gel stickers, which are MY FAVORITES!

"Those are *mine*!" I yell, reaching to try to take his construction paper. My hand grabs one corner, and it rips off a big chunk, but not a chunk with any of my stickers.

"Hey, hey, Mandy, sit down." Mrs. Spangle puts her hands on my shoulders and presses me back into my seat. "There's no screaming in this classroom. What's going on here?"

"Dennis," I begin, spitting his name out like it's a disease, "stole my sticker book, and now he's using my stickers."

Dennis shrugs his shoulders then, like this is

not a gigantic tragedy or anything. "I had to," he explains. "Because I didn't have a glue stick."

"If you need a glue stick, you borrow one from your neighbor," Mrs. Spangle says. "Or you ask me. You don't use Mandy's stickers."

"But Polka Dot stole my glue stick," Dennis says.

"No name-calling," Mrs. Spangle says. "Mandy, did you take Dennis's glue stick?"

"I borrowed it," I say honestly, "because he wouldn't let me use it and mine was empty. But he *stole* my sticker book."

"Hand them over, both of you." Mrs. Spangle holds out her hands. Dennis and I reach into our desks, and I pull out his glue stick, and Dennis removes my sticker book. We hand them both to Mrs. Spangle.

"Dennis, place this in your desk," she says, handing him the glue stick. "Mandy, take this sticker book home. No more sticker books in school. That goes for all of you." She looks around the room.

"But what about the stickers Dennis used?" I ask, pointing to his paper. "They're my favorites."

Mrs. Spangle helps me peel the gel stickers off of Dennis's construction paper, but she still writes my initials on the board for screaming, and she adds *DR* right underneath for Dennis's name, so that is something, I guess. Anya helps me reseal the stickers in my book, but their backs are now covered in construction paper fuzz and they don't stick as well as they used to.

I glare at Dennis before I walk my sticker book over to my cubby to place it in my book bag, and I feel tears tickling the back of my eyes. But I press my palms into them, because I am not going to cry like a big crybaby. I am not like Paige, after all.

CHAPTER 8

Screaming Fraidy Cats

PAIGE STAYS AT GRANDMOM'S FOR ANOTHER NIGHT IN A ROW, which makes me very happy. I wish Grandmom would take Timmy and the twins with her while she is at it. Even if Timmy is getting on my nerves a little less than usual this week, it would be nice to be rid of them all for just one night, so that I could pretend to be an only child again.

"Is Paige staying at Grandmom's until she goes home?" I ask Mom as I eat breakfast (which is cereal and not chocolate pudding or ketchup pizzas, and so it is not nearly as fun).

"No, she's coming back today while you're at school," Mom answers. "And now listen to me: I want you to be kind to Paige when she returns to our house. It's not easy to be away from home. It's your job to make her feel welcome, no matter how bossy you think she is. Plus, you can be pretty bossy yourself, you know."

"I am not—" I begin, but then I stop myself, because Mom is a little bit right. But not about the being away from home part, I think. "I like to be away from home."

"The only place you've ever stayed away from home is Grandmom's," Mom tells me.

"No, we slept at Uncle Rich's house before," I answer. "Before the twins were born."

"Right, but that was with me and Dad," Mom says. "It's not the same if your family is there."

"You said we're Paige's family."

"We are. But we're not her immediate family—I'm not her mom, Dad's not her father, you're not her sister," Mom explains. "In fact, she doesn't even know what it's like to have a sister. I'm sure it's hard for her to be away from what she knows."

"I don't think we're so bad," I say. "And anyway, I think she should learn what my name is. She keeps calling me Manda."

"I'll talk with her about that when she gets back this morning," Mom says. "I agree—that is something simple she can do for you, call you by the name you like. But I think you could make some compromises yourself. Remember how excited you were to have Paige visit? It bothers me that you two are wasting all this time when you could be having fun together."

"She's not as fun as she used to be," I tell Mom honestly.

"Promise me you'll try harder with her this

afternoon," Mom says. "I bet you'll find that the same Paige you liked before is still in there."

"I don't think so," I answer.

"You still want to go to the carnival with Grandmom on Friday, don't you?"

"Yes."

"Then you better try," Mom says. "Remember, you have to cook five dishes out of that cookbook Grandmom gave you. You wouldn't want Paige to get to go and not you."

And that is the truth, so when Mom goes into the twins' room, I scurry off of my chair and grab the cookbook from the pile on the counter. I run into the living room and stuff the book in my book bag, because there is no way I am going to let Paige get a head start.

Without any stickers to trade at school, I whip out the cookbook in the cubbies to show it to Anya.

"Why'd you bring that to school?" Natalie asks. "You can't cook here."

"I know." I say "know" extra loud because Natalie asks a lot of questions. "I brought it because I did not want Paige to cook out of it while I am at school. Because she might make five whole recipes, and then Grandmom will take her to the carnival without me, and that is not okay."

Anya takes the book from me and flips through the pages. "Ooh, these look great," she says, pointing to a picture of marshmallow ghosts. "And they should be easy to make—you just stick pretzel sticks in the marshmallows to hold them up, then use chocolate chips for the eyes and mouth. You could totally cook them."

"That's not really cooking," Natalie says. "You're just putting them together. It's more like a craft."

"I just have to make five things out of this

book," I tell her. "It doesn't matter how hard or easy they are. But I hate ghosts, so I don't really want to make those."

"Why do you hate ghosts?" Natalie asks.

"I think there's a ghost in my house," I answer. "I think it snuck in from the Packles' porch. They always put up a big ghost display on Halloween, and when they took it down, I think a ghost escaped."

Anya's and Natalie's eyes both grow wide at this story, and I feel goose bumps crawling up my arms just thinking about it.

"*Boo!*" a ghost calls from behind the curtain on the other side of the cubbies, and Anya, Natalie, and I all scream, though not as loudly as I did about the stickers. The ghost cackles a laugh at us, and then he appears from behind the curtain.

Only it is not a ghost at all. It is Dennis. Being terrible.

"Knock it off, Dennis!" I yell at him.

"Polka Dot's a fraidy cat," he says. "Fraidy cat, fraidy cat."

"Be quiet, Dennis," Anya says. "No one's talking to you. Go away."

Dennis makes haunting sounds and wiggles his arms in the air, trying to scare us again, before he finally leaves the cubbies. I take my cookbook back and toss it toward my book bag.

"This is why I can't make marshmallow ghosts," I explain. "Because ghosts are as horrible as Dennis."

Paige is sitting on the floor of the living room surrounded by the twins when I get home from school, so my afternoon is not off to a great start.

"Hi, Mandy," she greets me, and I am kind of shocked then, because Paige is finally calling me by the right name, so Mom must have had a talk with her about it.

"Hi," I answer, and I remember what Mom said about trying really hard to be nicer to Paige. "How was Grandmom's?"

"It was fun," Paige says. "Do you want to play with Samantha, Cody, and me?"

"I don't play with the twins," I answer. "Anyway, they are not even good at playing."

"Okay." Paige looks down and wiggles a rattle in front of one of the twins' faces, and she looks pretty sad about it actually.

"But," I continue, "if you want to cook with me out of that cookbook, I will. You know, so we can both go with Grandmom to the carnival."

"I'd like that." Paige nods. "Do you want to pick the recipe?"

"Yes." I nod my head and throw my book bag onto the couch to open it. I unzip the zipper and reach inside. I pull out my homework folder, my reading book, my pencil box, the Rainbow Sparkle windup toy that I am not supposed to bring to school, and seven ponytail holders.

But no cookbook.

I look inside the bag and can't see much in the

dark, so I turn the whole thing upside down and shake it.

Nothing.

"Oh no," I say. "Oh no, oh no, oh no."

"What is it?" Paige asks.

"The cookbook is missing."

"No, it's not, it's in the kitchen," Paige says. "Isn't it?"

"No, I brought it to school. But it's not in my book bag."

"Why did you bring it to school?"

"That is not important," I say. "The important part is that it was stolen."

"How do you know it was stolen?" Paige asks. "Maybe you lost it."

"I didn't lose it," I say. "I don't lose things. They get stolen." And I am absolutely positive I know who the cookbook thief is, and this time, I can't even blame a ghost.

CHAPTER 9

Ghost Hunting

"I THINK WE SHOULD TELL GRANDMOM," PAIGE SAYS. IT IS A whole hour after I discovered that the cookbook is missing, and we are sitting at the kiddie table in the toy room, deciding what to do. "If we tell her the book was stolen, then she can't expect us to cook five things out of it in two days."

"We already cooked the egg salad," I remind her, and I make a face because egg salad is still disgusting.

"Even so," Paige begins, "we won't be able to

cook anything else without recipes. We should tell her what happened to the book."

"But then she'll ask why I brought it to school," I say.

"Tell her you brought it for show-and-tell," Paige suggests, and this is not a bad plan.

I nod my head. "Maybe," I say. "But I bet Grandmom would like it better if we still tried to cook something without the book."

Paige thinks about this for one second. "You're probably right. But I don't remember any recipes off the top of my head."

"Come on," I say, and I stand up and scurry into the kitchen to open the pantry door. "I have an idea." I examine each shelf of the pantry until I find what I am looking for: a box of pretzel sticks, which has probably been wedged into the corner of the pantry since before the twins were born, because no one in this house really likes pretzels.

These sticks crunch so loudly when you bite them that they make my teeth hurt and scratch the top of my mouth, but finally, they are going to be put to good use.

"Do you see any marshmallows?" I ask.

"Your mom keeps marshmallows in the house?" Paige asks like she is shocked. "Mine doesn't."

"Sometimes," I say. "But when she does, they're usually hidden somewhere." Paige stands on her tippy toes, and it is very useful that she is ten years old and taller than me, because she spots it: a gigantic bag of marshmallows hiding behind the cans of green beans.

"Yes!" I yell. "Now we just need chocolate chips. Boost me onto the counter." I pull out one of the bottom drawers, which is filled with dish towels, and step on top of it, then I use my arms to get onto the counter while Paige pushes me up from behind. I kneel in front of Mom's baking cabinet, and I dig through the containers of flour and sugar until I find the bag of chocolate chips. "Got them!" I close the cabinet door and slide back down to the floor.

"Are you going to give me a hint about what we're making?" Paige asks.

"Marshmallow ghosts," I say. "Anya saw them in the cookbook—you know, before it was stolen—and I think I remember the recipe."

"Ooh, I hate ghosts," Paige says. "I think there's a ghost in my house." And my chin drops toward my chest.

"You have a ghost too?" I ask, and it comes out as sort of a squeak. I lower my voice then, because I do not want Mom to hear, and I whisper, "I am pretty sure there is a ghost in my house. I think it escaped from the Packles' Halloween porch."

Paige nods her head very seriously, like this

story makes absolute sense. "The ghost in my house smells like ranch dressing. Sometimes, when it's early in the morning and I'm the only one awake, I'll come downstairs and smell ranch dressing everywhere."

"Have you ever seen the ghost?"

"Nope," Paige answers. "Have you seen yours?"

"No," I say. "I do not want to either."

"Our ghosts must not be that scary though, right?" Paige asks. "I mean, don't you think they would have done something bad by now if they were?"

"I guess so," I say. "How do you think we can get rid of them?"

Paige pauses for a second, and then she lifts a single marshmallow out of the bag.

"By eating them, of course," she says with a smile, and she pops an entire marshmallow in her mouth, handing me one to do the same. We stuff our cheeks with marshmallows until we can't fit anymore inside, and we have to concentrate very hard on chewing so that we don't spit them out.

We then begin to use the marshmallows to create the ghosts. We stick the pretzel rods in the bottoms of them as a handle, and we push three chocolate chips into the sides of the marshmallows so that they look like the ghosts' eyes and mouths. When we each have one finished, we hold them up by their pretzel handles so they can speak to each other, like in a puppet show.

In my best spooky voice, I ask Paige, "What do you think they're going to do to us now?" while I wave my marshmallow ghost around like he is floating.

In an equally spooky voice, Paige answers, "I'm afraid they're going to bite our heads off," and then she sticks her entire marshmallow ghost inside her mouth and chomps down. I do the same to mine, and I am pretty sure these marshmallow ghosts are the best recipe I have ever made.

And for the first time all week, I remember why Paige truly is my favorite cousin.

* * *

"Dennis stole my cookbook," I say to Anya the minute I see her at school the next morning. "He took it out of my book bag."

"No way," Anya says. "He is terrible."

"Will you help me get it back?" I ask.

"Of course," Anya answers, and this is why she is my favorite person in the world. "I'll go distract him. You look in his book bag."

"What if it's not in there?" I ask.

"Then we'll check his desk."

"What if he took it home?"

"I bet he didn't," Anya says. "You stay here." She points toward Dennis's cubby. "When you see me talking to him, make your move into the book bag."

I hide behind the curtain in the cubbies and watch Anya walk over to Dennis's desk. She stands behind his chair so that Dennis has to turn around to talk to her and is facing away from the cubbies. Anya is pretty much a genius, I think.

As fast as my legs can go, I run over to Dennis's cubby and unzip his bag. I don't like touching Dennis's things because they are covered in all his gross Dennis germs, but this is an emergency. I open the book bag as wide as I can and look inside.

"Yuck," I say. Dennis's bag is filled with dirty tissues and candy wrappers and bottle caps and action figures (which he is not supposed to have in school) and a bunch of other dumb boy things.

But no cookbook.

I stuff his bag back in his cubby and march straight over to his desk. I do not even care about Anya's plan anymore, because I am furious.

"Give it back," I say as soon as I reach him, and I say each word like there is a period after it.

"What are you talking about, Polka Dot?" Dennis responds.

"Give it back," I say. "I know you have it."

"I don't know what you're talking about."

"GIVE. IT. BACK!" I am yelling now. "It's very important!"

"I told you, I don't know what you're talking about!" Dennis answers. "I didn't take any of your ugly things."

I step right over to Dennis so I am standing above his Mohawk, and I push my way toward his desk. I look inside and begin dumping out all of the contents—folders and notebooks and crinkled-up papers and dried-up markers and dusty raisins. They hit the floor one right after the other as Dennis scrambles to catch them.

"Mandy! MANDY!" I whirl around at the sound of Mrs. Spangle's voice. "What on earth is the problem *now*?"

"Dennis stole my cookbook," I explain. "My grandmother gave it to me, and it is very important, and I need it back now or else I won't get to go to the carnival with my cousin, and he *stole* it."

"I didn't steal it!" Dennis yells back. "I promise! Mrs. Spangle, I didn't."

"Mandy, when was the last time you saw your cookbook?"

"Yesterday," I say. "I had to bring it to school because I didn't want my cousin to cook out of it without me, because then Grandmom would have brought her to the carnival and not me, so I had it in my book bag and I was showing it to Anya and Natalie, and now it's GONE."

"See, this is why I don't like you bringing things that are important to you to school," Mrs. Spangle says. "But since that ship has already sailed, did you check your cubby?"

"Yes," I answer.

"Did you look really well?"

"Yes."

"Are you sure?"

"No."

Mrs. Spangle sighs at me then. "Go look. Natalie, can you help her? I know you're very organized about these kinds of things." Natalie stands up and walks with me to the cubbies. We take every single item out of my cubby, and guess what? Still no cookbook.

"It's not here!" I call across the room.

"Whose cubbies are on either side of yours?" Mrs. Spangle asks.

"Julia's and Anya's," I answer.

"Julia and Anya, do me a favor and go look around your cubbies and see if you find Mandy's cookbook," Mrs. Spangle tells them. "Sometimes things wander into the wrong cubby by accident."

Julia and Anya join Natalie and me in the

cubbies, and they root through their things. Anya pulls her book bag and jacket out of her cubby, and then both of us stand as still as statues and stare.

We stare at the cookbook that is lying upside down at the bottom of her cubby.

My cookbook.

"How'd that get in there?" Anya whispers to me.

"I don't know," I say. "Maybe I put it in the wrong cubby?" Anya reaches down and picks up the book, and she tries to give it to me quickly before Mrs. Spangle can see.

"What's that you have there, Anya?" Mrs. Spangle asks.

"We found it," she calls back. "It was in my cubby by mistake."

"Oh, it was, was it?" Mrs. Spangle says. "I think that means you have something to say to Dennis, doesn't it, Mandy?"

I stare back at Mrs. Spangle but do not say one

word. Instead, I stuff the cookbook into my own book bag and make sure that it is safely put away before returning to my seat.

"We're waiting," Mrs. Spangle says to me. "What do you say to Dennis for accusing him of stealing your book?"

"Sorry," I answer, though I do not really mean it. After all, it is not like Dennis hasn't stolen any of my things before. Just because he didn't take this one thing shouldn't mean I have to apologize for it.

"You know, you two are more alike than you want to realize," Mrs. Spangle tells us. "If you would just try to get along, I bet you might actually like each other. Now, Mandy, help Dennis pick up all of the things you dumped out of his desk while I put your initials on the board. And, Dennis, this is a good opportunity for you to clean up the trash that you're keeping in there, don't you think?"

Mrs. Spangle walks away, and I kneel next to Dennis's desk and start lifting all of his gross things off of the floor.

"See what you get for being a tattletale, Polka Dot?" Dennis whispers to me, and I roll my eyes up to the ceiling at him.

Even though a small part of me knows that Dennis is right. Because tattletales never win.

CHAPTER 10

Paige Times Two

AS SOON AS I GET HOME FROM SCHOOL, I THROW MY BOOK bag onto the couch, unzip the zipper, remove the cookbook, and yell, "PAIGE!"

"I'm up here," Paige calls from the top of the stairs. I run over to the bottom so I can face her.

"Come on," I say. "I got the cookbook back. If we work really fast, I bet we can make three more things before Grandmom comes for dinner."

"Fabulous," Paige says, and she bounds down

the stairs and follows me into the kitchen. I whip open the book, and we stare at the table of contents.

"We should probably see what ingredients we have first, right?" Paige asks. "So we know what we can make?"

"Nah. If we don't have it, we'll just use something else. That's what I did with my pizzas. I used ketchup instead of tomato sauce, and it was the best pizza I ever had."

"Ooh, how about these?" Paige points to a picture in the book. "Sandwiches with chocolate-hazelnut spread and raspberries. They look pretty."

"We don't have any of that stuff except the bread," I say, opening the refrigerator door. "But how about . . . sandwiches with peanut butter and apples? That is almost the same thing."

"Perfect," Paige answers. "You're really good at this."

"I know," I agree. "I've had a lot of practice not getting what I want."

"Really? It seems like you always make sure you get what you want. It's kind of impressive."

I shake my head back and forth. "No. Timmy gets what he wants, and the twins get whatever they want because, if they don't, they'll just cry about it," I explain. "I have to compromise all the time." "Compromising" is what Mom says I have to do whenever she thinks I am being a brat. It is one of my least favorite words ever.

"You're lucky—you don't have to compromise at your house," I continue. "Because you don't have any brothers and sisters getting what they want instead of you."

"That's true," Paige says as she spreads a mound of peanut butter across a slice of bread. "But sometimes I think it would be fun to have a brother or sister, at least for a little while.

That's why I like coming to your house."

I think about this for a moment. "So who is your favorite cousin now? Timmy?"

"You'll always be my favorite cousin," Paige says. "You know why?"

"Why?"

"Because you are fabulous," Paige tells me, and she swipes a smear of peanut butter across the tip of my nose. I stick my tongue as far out of my mouth as it will go, seeing if I can lick it, and Paige laughs so hard at me that she has to sit on the floor for a minute, holding her belly.

"Well, it sounds like someone is having fun in here," Mom says. "Nice nose, Mand."

I wipe the rest of the peanut butter off of my nose with a paper towel. "We are going to make the rest of the dishes before Grandmom comes for dinner. We still have time, right?"

"Sure. I'm glad to see you two enjoying each

other's company again," Mom says. "Just call me if you need to use the oven or to cut something with a knife. Don't try to do it yourselves. And, girls?"

We both turn around and look at Mom, waiting.

"Have fun!" she says.

"We will," I say, "because we're family. Right, Paige?"

"Family *and* friends," Paige responds, "which is even better. Now let's see what else we can cook." And I do not even care anymore that Paige can still be a little bit bossy, because she said I was fabulous, and you know what?

She is pretty fabulous too.

Dad brings home pizza for dinner, even after Paige and I spent all afternoon working in the kitchen.

"You two can serve the appetizers and dessert," Mom tells us.

"What did you make? It looks delicious," Grandmom asks.

Paige and I present our peanut butter and apple sandwiches and our lettuce and tomato pita tacos for appetizers, then our marshmallow ghosts, blueberry and chocolate yogurts, and banana and gummy bear sundaes for dessert.

"We made an extra dish," I tell Grandmom. "Since you and I didn't get to eat the egg salad."

"The gummy bear sundaes were Mandy's idea," Paige explains.

"Why am I not surprised?" Grandmom responds. "Well, girls, I'm very proud of you. I like how you worked together to create all of these dishes yourselves—that took a lot of work."

"So do we get to go to the carnival tomorrow?" I ask, because I do not know why Grandmom is holding her horses about telling us.

"Yes," Grandmom says. "I'll pick you two

up first thing in the morning. How does that sound?"

"Fabulous!" Paige and I answer at the same time, which makes us laugh at ourselves.

"Jinx." Paige holds out her pinky toward mine.

"What does that do?"

"We said the same thing at the same time. Now we have to lock our pinkies and say 'jinx,'" she explains.

"Like a pinky swear?"

"Exactly like a pinky swear."

I wrap my pinky around Paige's and we call out "jinx," and then I take an enormous spoonful of my banana and gummy bear sundae, without the bananas. "Wahoo!" I call out when my mouth is full, and drips of ice cream fly out of my mouth. This makes Paige laugh all over again, though Mom and Dad do not think it is so funny.

That night I hear Paige breathing quietly on the bouncy mattress on my floor, but I cannot fall asleep because I am too excited. Instead, I lie in my bed and stare up at the ceiling, thinking about the roller coasters and games that I am going to see tomorrow and how I am going to get to spend the whole day with Paige and Grandmom, with no Timmy and no twins getting in the way.

Grandmom says that the carnival is the only place where it's okay to eat cotton candy before breakfast, so Paige and I share a gigantic pink fluffy mound, and I think it is delicious, even though I usually hate pink things.

"Now can we go on the roller coaster?" I ask. I have never been on the carnival's roller coaster, because I thought it was scary when I was little, but now I do not, because I am not a fraidy cat.

"Yes, can we?" Paige asks.

"I don't know," Grandmom begins. "Roller coasters aren't really my thing."

"It does not even look too scary, though," I tell her. "It's not like the big roller coasters with loops and stuff."

"I think my roller coaster days are over," Grandmom tells us. "But if you two want to go together, you can. I'll wait for you at the exit."

"Really?" Paige looks at Grandmom and then at me. "Are you ready?"

"Yes, absolutely," I answer, and I grab her hand to run to the roller coaster line.

"Stay together!" Grandmom calls after us. The roller coaster worker measures us to make sure we are both tall enough, and when we are, we join the back of the line.

"This is amazing," Paige says. "I never get to go on roller coasters because my parents don't like them but won't let me ride by myself."

"I don't think they would be very fun by yourself anyway," I tell her. "The best part of a roller coaster is getting to scream as loud as you want, and that is only fun to do when there is someone next to you."

Paige nods her head in agreement, and when it is our turn, we board our roller coaster car side by side.

"I'm a little scared," Paige confesses then.

"You will love it," I tell her. "Now put your hands in the air. This makes a roller coaster even better, I think." The ride takes off with a start, and the wind smacks me in the face. My hair flies behind me as I keep my hands raised all the way above my head, and every time the roller coaster lurches down a hill, I scream, and Paige does the same.

When the ride grinds to a stop, I look over at

Paige, who is smiling almost as widely as I am, her hair covering her face like a gigantic mop.

"That was amazing!" she calls out.

"Do you want to go again?" I ask.

"Umm," Paige says as we step out of our car, pushing our hair away from our faces. "Can we take a little break? I think I had too much cotton candy to ride two times in a row."

"Sure," I tell her, and we skip over to Grandmom, who is waiting for us right by the exit. "What should we do now?"

"How about," Paige begins, "I try to win you a goldfish?"

"Really? Can you? Do you know how?" I ask.

"I told you, my parents won't let me go on the roller coaster at our town's carnival, so I spend a lot of time playing the games," she tells me. "I'm pretty good at the one with the fishbowls."

"But won't you want to keep the fish?" I ask her.

"And take it in the car all the way back to my house?" she says. "Nah, if I win one, you can have it."

"Okay, let's do it!" I say, and Paige and I run ahead of Grandmom to the goldfish game. Sure enough, on her very first try, Paige throws the little ball directly into one of the fishbowls, and I am pretty sure I have never cheered so loudly in my life.

"Here you go, sweetheart." The worker gives Paige a plastic bag with a bright orange goldfish swimming inside, and Paige hands the bag right over to me. I throw my arm that is not holding the bag around Paige's neck for a hug, being careful not to slosh my new fish around too much.

"What are you going to name him?" she asks.

"How do you know it's a boy?"

"I don't," Paige answers. "Maybe it's a girl."

"Then I will name her Paige," I say. "After my favorite cousin." I lift up the bag then so I can kiss the side of it, since I am so glad this goldfish is mine.

"Wahoo!" I call out, looping the arm with the goldfish through Paige's elbow, and reaching out my other hand toward Grandmom. We weave through the carnival, and I hold both of them close to me so we are all together. Because one of the best parts of relatives is that they belong to you, and if you're really lucky, one of them will always think that you are the most fabulous person in your family.

Mandy's Lessons:

1. LEFTOVER PUDDING IS BETTER THAN NO PUDDING AT ALL.
2. COUSINS ARE GREAT UNLESS YOU DO NOT LIKE THEM.
3. NEVER INVITE AN EXTRA PERSON ON A PLAYDATE.
4. GRANDMOMS LOVE ALL GRANDKIDS THE SAME, WHICH IS ANNOYING.
5. PIZZA IS THE BEST BREAKFAST.
6. EVEN IF YOUR BROTHER STINKS, HE IS STILL YOURS.
7. IT IS POSSIBLE TO MAKE A BIG KID CRY.
8. DON'T ACT LIKE A FRAIDY CAT IF YOU DON'T WANT TO BE CALLED ONE.
9. GHOSTS DON'T LIKE IT WHEN YOU BITE THEIR HEADS OFF.
10. IT IS NO FUN TO RIDE A ROLLER COASTER BY YOURSELF.

DON'T MISS MANDY'S FIRST ADVENTURE,

DON'T WEAR

PolKa-Dot Underwear

WITH WHITE PANTS

(AND OTHER LESSONS I'VE LEARNED)!

I KEEP TELLING MOM ABOUT THE WHITE PANTS, and she says to wear them anyway.

"They will make me fall down," I explain.

"Pants do not make you fall down, Amanda," Mom answers, because she does not understand anything at all.

"Yes, they do." I stomp my foot and cross my arms and put on my very best "I am pouting now" face. "White pants like dirt, and they will make me fall in it."

"Then be extra careful at recess, please," Mom says, holding the awful pants open for me to step in.

"No."

Mom sighs a big gust of breath in my face and stares at me with her "I mean business" eyes. "Amanda Berr, I am going to count to three."

"I will get ketchup on them," I say.

"One . . ."

"I will drop marker on them," I say.

"Two . . ."

I groan like a dinosaur and lift up one leg just so Mom will stop counting.

"Here is a deal," I begin. "I will wear these awful white pants if you buy me periwinkle pants." My favorite color is periwinkle. It is more beautiful than blue and more perfect than purple and it is a fun name to say. But I do not have one piece of periwinkle clothing, and I think this is

unfair. I checked my whole entire closet—shirts and shorts and dresses and ugly fancy blouses that Mom keeps in plastic until Easter. No periwinkle. I had held my periwinkle crayon from my box of 152 colors up to each piece, just to be sure. And still nothing.

"I'll look for some," Mom says, shaking the white pants in front of me.

"Today," I insist. "I want periwinkle pants today."

"I cannot get you periwinkle pants today," Mom says. "Why can't you just like a nice, normal color—like pink? How about if I get you pink pants?"

"I hate pink."

"Good, *these* pants aren't pink." Mom shakes the pants even more ferociously.

I grab the pants in my own two hands then. "I will dress myself. I am not a baby," I say.

"Fine," Mom answers. "Be downstairs and dressed in five minutes, Amanda. And in *those* pants. I don't have time for any more funny business today."

So I stuff my legs into the pants and stomp down to the kitchen table, and Mom does not even say, *Thank you for wearing the awful white pants, Mandy.* Mandy is my real name even though Mom thinks it is Amanda. I do not like the name "Amanda" because it does not have any Ys in it, and this is a tragedy. I like to make Ys with curlicue tails and I cannot do this when there are no Y's in my name, so this is why my name is Mandy and *not* Amanda.

"Finish up your cereal, Amanda," Mom says. "Your bus will be at the corner in ten minutes. Hurry."

"I cannot hurry because of these pants," I tell her.

"Don't be ridiculous," Mom responds, which I think is pretty rude, if I am being honest.

"I am being serious," I insist. "If I eat quickly, I will dump the cereal onto the pants and they will be dirty because white pants love dirt. I told you so already." I lift one kernel of cereal onto my spoon very slowly and raise it toward my mouth, just to show Mom how careful I have to be.

"If you want to eat that way, it's up to you," Mom says. "But you only have five more minutes to do so, Amanda."

"Mandy," I remind her, but she does not correct herself. Mom is not such a good listener. She was not such a good listener ever, but she is even worse now that the twins are here. Everything in this house for the past five months has been about the twins:

"The twins are hungry."

"Don't be noisy, you'll wake the twins."

"Aren't the twins adorable?"

The twins are not adorable. They're damp. "Damp" is my new favorite word—my teacher, Mrs. Spangle, taught it to us during our science lesson. It means when something is just a little bit wet. And the twins are always just a little bit wet. Their diapers are wet or their drool is wet or their food is wet. They're damp. Like that washcloth that is still damp the next morning even though it's had the whole entire night to dry from your bath. And damp things are gross, I've decided.

Mom says it's not nice to call the twins "gross." She says I have to call them "Samantha and Cody," but most of the time, she's not paying enough attention to see if I do, so I don't.

My little brother Timmy also hardly gets any attention anymore, but I don't mind that so much. Because he's pretty gross too.

"Oof, Cody is wet again." Mom pats the diaper on one of the twins and lifts him up. He starts to wail then, because all the twins like to do is cry and get even damper.

They are pretty terrible, if I am being honest.

"Amanda, can you get yourself to your bus stop?" Mom calls over her shoulder on her way to the twins' room.

"I'm eight," I answer, because Mom forgets that I am not a baby. I know important things like how to get to my bus stop and how to read books without pictures in them and how to cook—well, to pour cereal, which is pretty much the same thing.

"Don't forget your lunch box!" Mom calls from the twins' room. "It's on the counter." I swirl the rest of my cereal around in the bowl and try to splash a little on my pants so I can change them. "Hurry, Amanda!"

I groan like a dinosaur again and pick my

Rainbow Sparkle lunch box up off the counter. Rainbow Sparkle is who I want to be when I grow up: She is fast and she is funny and she has purple eyes, which is what I want to have (hers are almost periwinkle, only not quite). I'm stuck with brown eyes and brown hair, when all I want are beautiful purple eyes and silky white hair like Rainbow Sparkle's.

Rainbow Sparkle is a cat, if I forgot to mention. She has her own show on TV.

"You can't become a cartoon cat when you grow up," Mom always says. She really does not understand anything at all.

"I'm leaving!" I yell to Mom as I head for the front door. On my way I see my stuffed Rainbow Sparkle sitting underneath the coffee table, and I cram her into my lunch box even though one of Mrs. Spangle's rules is "No toys in school." I am going to need Rainbow Sparkle to protect me from these pants. Because Rainbow Sparkle is the only white-colored thing in the whole universe that is not awful.

Mrs. Spangle looks like a porcupine, but she is nicer. Porcupines stick people with their quills and Mrs. Spangle has red hair that looks like quills, but she does not stick people with it. I know this because I touched Mrs. Spangle's hair once and it did not stick me. It did feel a little bit prickly at the top, but it was soft when I rubbed my hand over it.

"Please don't pet me, Mandy," Mrs. Spangle had said, so I have not touched her hair again, even though sometimes I would like to.

I am thinking about petting Mrs. Spangle's hair while she stands at the front of our room and tells us about our big second-grade Presidential Pageant.

"The president's coming?" I call out.

"Mandy," Mrs. Spangle says with a warning in her voice. Mrs. Spangle has seven big rules for our classroom, and I am pretty good at following three of them. "No calling out" is number four on the list, and that is not one of my favorites.

I cover my mouth with one hand and shoot the other one in the air.

"Yes, Mandy?" Mrs. Spangle calls on me.

"The president's coming?"

"That's a good guess, but no," Mrs. Spangle answers. I slide down in my chair and slouch, disappointed. "Instead of having one president visit, you're all going to become presidents for the day!"

And I hate to say it after I made the big deal with the slouch and all, but this is just about the best news I've ever heard.

"Wahoo!" I leap up from my chair and pump

my fist in the air. Luckily, three other kids do this too, except without the "wahoo."

I sit back in my chair and raise my hand as quickly as I can. I place my left hand over my mouth, just to remind myself to keep it closed until Mrs. Spangle calls on me.

"Yes, Mandy?" Mrs. Spangle says, so I snap my left hand away from my mouth.

"Can I be George Washington?" George Washington is clearly the best president because he was first, and I always like to be first. I was born first in my family, so it only seems fair.

"I'll be assigning your parts for the assembly next week," Mrs. Spangle says. "In the meantime, we're going to get caught up on our presidential knowledge each day, so you'll all get to learn about the presidents who might not be as famous as George Washington or Abraham Lincoln."

I shoot my hand into the air again.

"Yes, Mandy?"

"I would like to be George Washington, please," I say. I use "please" and everything, because that is one of Mrs. Spangle's rules that I am good at: "Be polite."

"Everyone will find out next week," Mrs. Spangle says. "Now let's get our things and line up for lunch. Natalie's table first." Natalie's table always gets to be first because Natalie sits with her hands folded all the time and she makes her whole table do the same. Natalie is no fun at all, if I forgot to mention.

When it is finally my table's turn, I grab my Rainbow Sparkle lunch box out of my cubby and stand behind Anya. We walk in a not-so-straight line to the cafeteria, and I plop my lunch box on top of the table so that it makes as loud a noise as possible. Natalie gives me a dirty look and covers her ears, but Anya slams her lunch box on the table right next to mine, even louder than I did.

Anya is my favorite person in the world, at least most of the time.

I like Anya because both "Amanda" and "Anya" begin with the letter *A* and end with the letter *A*, which is kind of amazing. Of course, Amanda has another *A* in the middle, so my name is a little better, but Anya's is pretty good too. (And Anya gets to have a *Y* in her name all the time, which makes me a little bit jealous.)

Plus, Anya likes being loud and she likes Rainbow Sparkle's TV show, so we have a lot to talk about.

"Do you know Dennis hid my lunch box in the cubbies again?" Anya asks. Dennis sits next to Anya in Mrs. Spangle's class, and she has a lot of problems with him because he is horrible.

I look over at the boys' cafeteria table and

glare at Dennis. Dennis has a Mohawk in his hair and so many freckles on his nose that you can barely see it at all.

"Leave Anya alone, Freckle Face!" I yell at him, but he doesn't hear me. That is probably for the best, because another one of Mrs. Spangle's rules is "No name-calling." But Freckle Face is just such a perfect name-call for Dennis.

Though I've always kind of wanted to have some freckles myself, if I am being honest.

Anya shrugs. "Don't worry about him," she says. "I'll tell Mrs. Spangle if he does it again, and then he'll have to miss recess."

Recess. Recess is the best time ever. Anya and I have been playing Squash the Lemon on the slide with some other girls, which is not really allowed because the lunch aides think we are going to squash each other to death, but we play until they blow the whistle about it.

I open my lunch box very carefully so that Rainbow Sparkle does not fall out. If Natalie sees her, she will tell Mrs. Spangle about it because Natalie is the police of Mrs. Spangle's rules. I give Rainbow Sparkle a quick pat on the nose so she does not feel left out, pull out my food, and then slam my lunch box shut real quick.

"Shh." Natalie gives me a not-nice look through her glasses, and I give her my best "You are driving me bananas" face. Dad taught me the "You are driving me bananas" face, but I do it better than him, I think.

I unwrap my sandwich and find peanut butter and jelly, which is my favorite. Except this sandwich has strawberry jam, and I keep telling bad-listener Mom that I hate strawberry jam because it has seeds. I like grape jelly only, because grape jelly is purple, which is almost like periwinkle. Plus, no seeds.

Also, jam is slippery and slimy, and now I have these white pants and I can't get any strawberry on them.

"Ugh," I groan real loud so my whole table can hear.

"What's wrong?" Anya asks. I point to my sandwich and make a face.

"Oh no, seeds," she says, and this is one reason why Anya is my favorite person in the world.

I bite into my sandwich as neatly as possible, making sure to hold the whole thing over the table and not over my pants. It takes a very long time to eat this way. So long that I don't even have a chance to eat my carrot sticks, but I didn't want to eat them anyway, so this is not a tragedy.

I always tell Mom that I want gummy bears in my lunch instead of carrot sticks, and she says this is not possible because gummy bears are not healthy. But gummy bears taste like fruit and they are delicious, so I do not know what the big deal is.

I line up behind Anya to hit the playground, and when we are allowed to go outside, I make a beeline for the slide. Three other girls from our class are already waiting at the bottom of the slide's ladder, ready to play our not-allowed game until the lunch aides come out of the cafeteria.

"Let's go, let's go, hurry!" I call. Everyone starts climbing to the top of the slide. The first girl slides down the normal way and plants her feet firmly in the dirt at the bottom. The next girl gets into position at the top, hanging each of her legs off either side of the slide. When she reaches the bottom, she slams into the first girl and they both grunt. And this is why Squash the Lemon is the best recess game ever.

Natalie slides down the same way, and then Anya. I am next.

"Do *not* go fast, Mandy," Natalie calls back to

me. "I can hardly breathe." Now, this makes no sense at all, because the whole point of Squash the Lemon is to go fast and squish people. So I start making my way to the top of the ladder so I can give them all the biggest slam they've ever had.

"Ready or not, here I come!" I call from the top of the slide, and I decide to go extra fast just for Natalie.

"Ewww!" I hear behind me. "Ewww!" I turn around and see Dennis and three of his silly boy friends standing at the bottom of the ladder.

"What do you want, Freckle Face?"

"Ewww, I can see your underwear," Dennis says. "Ewww!"

I was not expecting this.

I quickly feel around the back of my pants, making sure that the band of my underwear is not peeking out the top. It is not.

"Liar!" I yell at Dennis.

"Mandy wears polka-dot underwear," Dennis says in a singsong voice, and if I were not standing at the top of a slide right now, I promise I would tackle him.

Especially because I'm pretty sure that I *am* wearing polka-dot underwear.

How does he know that?

"Mandy wears polka-dot underwear," Dennis repeats. "You can see it through her pants."

All this commotion breaks up the squashing of the lemons at the bottom of the slide, and Anya and the other girls come around to see why Dennis is yelling. Anya looks up at me, and her eyes grow as wide as pancakes. She motions for me to get off the slide, real small so Dennis can't see.

I look down the ladder but decide that the slide itself is my fastest way off. So I shimmy to the bottom, which isn't even very fun because there is no one to squash. Anya is there to meet me.

"You can see your underwear through your pants," she whispers to me. "I think it's the sun." Anya hurries me off to stand under the oak tree in the shade, somewhere my polka dots will stay hidden.

And at this moment there are three things that I am furious at: Dennis, Mom, and these awful white pants.

Anya gives me her sweater to wear over my bottom for the rest of recess, and this is another reason why she is my favorite person in the world. When we get back to our classroom, I stuff my lunch box into my cubby and pop right up to Mrs. Spangle's desk before she can say I am not allowed.

"I need to tell you a secret," I say quietly.

"Not now, Mandy," Mrs. Spangle says. "It's time for—"

"It's an emergency," I interrupt her. "Emergency" is the kind of word that gets grown-ups to listen to you. "Broken" and "stain" and "dropped on his head" are also good words for this, I've learned.

"What is it?"

"I need to take off my underwear." I whisper this sentence real quietly in Mrs. Spangle's ear, and I think I spit on her a little bit.

"What do you mean? Did you have an accident?"

I shake my head. "My mom made me wear these awful white pants, and so everyone can see my underwear." I say this part super whispery too. "Dennis saw them on the playground."

"Stand back a second," Mrs. Spangle says, so I follow her directions and take one step back, because I am very good at listening to Mrs. Spangle's "Follow directions" rule. "Don't worry, I can't see anything."

"Look harder," I say, taking another step back, which means I have to talk a little bit louder. "What do you see now?"

"Nope, nothing," Mrs. Spangle answers. "You're safe."

I take one more step back, just to make sure. "Are you absolutely positive you can't see my underwear? They're polka dot." I accidentally say this real loud because I forgot about my super-whispery voice. And who appears at Mrs. Spangle's desk right at this moment but Dennis, and he laughs.

"I promise, Mandy," Mrs. Spangle says. "Take a seat, please, and get ready for math. Dennis, you too." Mrs. Spangle gives him a look like he is in trouble, but she does not write his initials on the board, which I think is unfair. If I had laughed about Dennis's underwear, I am absolutely positive I would have gotten my initials on the board, so I stick my tongue out at him.

"Hey, Natalie," Dennis says as he sits down. "Did you know Mandy is wearing polka-dot underwear?"

"So?" is all that Natalie answers. And sometimes I am very happy that Natalie is so dull. Because boring people do not care about things like polka-dot underwear.

I sit at my desk, but I keep Anya's sweater tied around my waist for the rest of the afternoon, and Anya does not even complain once that she is cold.

This is why I like Anya almost as much as I like Rainbow Sparkle and almost as much as I like fruity gummy bears. I could eat a gummy bear or twenty right now. Because gummy bears never, ever come in polka dot.